'I'd forgotten just how lovely you are.'

Perversely, Jo was cross with Alex. Surely he didn't expect to go straight back and pick up where they had left off? She blushed, and looked away.

'I'm sorry, I've embarrassed you. OK, no more personal remarks, and I'll do my best not to remember how you felt in my arms, if you could manage to wear something shapeless, put a bag over your head and not look at me with those wide and wicked eyes!'

Dear Reader

This month Caroline Anderson begins a trilogy detailing the loves of three women who work with children and babies at the Audley Memorial Hospital. PLAYING THE JOKER opens with Jo, whose traumatic past she must keep from Alex—a deeply emotional read. Margaret Barker takes us to Bali, while James plans to snare Marnie in SURGEON'S STRATEGY by Drusilla Douglas, and Jenna Reid finds her looks deny her the man she wants in Patricia Robertson's HEART IN JEOPARDY.

Enjoy!

The Editor

Caroline Anderson's nursing career was brought to an abrupt halt by a back injury, but her interest in medical things led her to work first as a medical secretary, and then, after completing her teacher training, as a lecturer in medical office practice to trainee medical secretaries. In addition to writing, she also runs her own business from her home in rural Suffolk, where she lives with her husband, two daughters, mother and dog.

Recent titles by the same author:

A PERFECT HERO
A GENTLE GIANT

PLAYING THE JOKER

BY

CAROLINE ANDERSON

MILLS & BOON LIMITED
ETON HOUSE   18–24 PARADISE ROAD
RICHMOND   SURREY   TW9 1SR

Many thanks to the Terrence Higgins Trust,
Positively Women, Carol, and many others,
for their help and information.
This book is dedicated to anyone whose
life has been touched by Aids.

First published in Great Britain 1992
by Mills & Boon Limited

© Caroline Anderson 1992

Australian copyright 1992
Philippine copyright 1992
This edition 1992

ISBN 0 263 77947 5

Set in 10 on 12 pt Linotron Times
03-9212-51660

Typeset in Great Britain by Centracet, Cambridge
Made and printed in Great Britain

CHAPTER ONE

'EXCUSE me a moment.'

The man seated behind the desk stretched out a hand and picked up the phone, his manner briskly professional as he dealt with the caller.

'Davie—yes, Jo. Ah, right—can you fill me in?' There was a pencil-tapping pause. 'I see—how many weeks is she?'

The other man stood up and walked over to the window, his warm brown eyes scanning the view with interest. The office—soon to be his office—was at the rear of the building on the third floor of what was apparently known affectionately as the Stork's Nest, the six-storey maternity block that overlooked the rest of the hospital and the woodland beyond.

The trees were rich and green, but it would soon be September and then, as the nights drew in, the leaves would blaze with colour, giving way in time to the stark beauty of winter and then the bright, soft fullness of spring.

God knew he was ready for some beauty and fullness in his life.

'Right, that's that. Shall we go down for coffee and meet the team?'

Alexander Carter straightened his tie, drew back his shoulders and gave Davie a brief nod.

'Thank you.'

He followed the man through the door, down the

stairs and along a wide, busy hospital corridor to the staff canteen and coffee lounge.

'There is a consultants' dining-room, but in practice very few of us use it—the food's the same, but it lacks the ambience.'

'I can imagine.' He glanced around him at the laughing crowd that seemed to shift and flow with a life of its own. 'It's popular.'

Owen Davie laughed. 'It's eleven o'clock—everyone's come for their fix of caffeine. Ah, here's part of the team. Allow me to introduce you. Dr Anne Gabriel, your SHO, and Dr Maggie Wells, paediatric SHO. You'll be seeing a lot of each other, I imagine. Ladies, this is Alexander Carter, who'll be taking over from me from Monday.'

As his mouth made the usual and accepted noises, Alex's eyes registered and catalogued the two women—Anne Gabriel, his SHO, a little brown mouse of a woman, her face remarkable only for its guarded expression and a certain wistfulness in the wide hazel eyes, and Maggie Wells, the paediatrician, her long red-blonde hair tied over one shoulder, her deep blue eyes in her fragile-seeming face bright and alert, assessing him with interest. They were both slightly on the small side of average, but, where Maggie was full of coiled energy and youthful enthusiasm, Anne, although slimmer, was somehow fuller, more mature—a woman to Maggie's girl. He glanced at her ring finger and saw it was empty—not that that necessarily meant anything these days, but he was curious. She would, after all, be working very closely with him over the next few months at least.

They chatted for a few minutes, but first Maggie's

bleep and then Anne's called them away, and he was left alone with Owen Davie. The man turned to him.

'Your senior registrar won't be here for a few minutes; she's admitting a patient from one of the antenatal clinics at the moment. Perhaps I should warn you about her. She's a very good doctor, but given to rather radical tendencies. We've had a few minor barneys over procedure on occasion, but nothing drastic. I think you should know, though, that she applied for my job. Her age and lack of experience went against her, but given time and the moderation of maturity she should be an excellent consultant one day. In fact, if it hadn't been for you, she might well have been given the post.'

Alex frowned. He really didn't want to start with staffing difficulties. 'Do you think she'll work for me, or do you think she'll look for another job?' he asked.

'Oh, I'm almost certain she'll stay. I'm only telling you this because you might find her a little resentful, but she's very professional in a rather off-the-wall kind of way, and she knows she'll get promotion soon enough. She's just a bit of a wild card—the joker in the pack, you might say. Ah, here she is now—Dr Harding!'

Alex looked across the room towards the doorway, and saw a tall, elegant woman with flaming dark red hair tumbling down her shoulders. Her back was towards them, her white coat flung over her arm, her body clad in a figure-hugging bottle-green linen dress that was belted in to her narrow waist with a broad cinch of scarlet. Her body was slender but lush, her curves full of promise, but it was that unbelievable hair that drew him.

Perhaps it was just wishful thinking that made her seem familiar—achingly, intimately familiar—but then she threw back her head and laughed, and, as she did so, she turned away from her companions and strode towards them on impossibly high heels.

Alex felt as if he'd been kicked in the gut. His heart crashed against his ribs, his tongue felt so thick that he thought he would choke on it, and a heavy surge of desire tautened his body with recognition.

As she met his eyes, her impossibly long legs faltered, but then she was there at his side, those fascinating aquamarine eyes wide with wariness and something else—regret?—but not before they had registered a leap of joy. She hadn't changed, except perhaps to add the lustre of maturity to already perfect features. Her skin looked unbelievably soft, smooth and rich like pale cream under the faint scatter of freckles. But perhaps she had changed, just slightly. He sensed rather than saw a touch of sadness in her that hadn't been there before.

'Joanna, allow me to introduce you to my replacement, Alexander Carter. Mr Carter, this is Dr Harding, your senior registrar.'

He held out his hand. 'It's good to see you again, Jo.'

She was stunned. She had been miles away, her mind on her clinic, when Owen Davie had reminded her that the new man was there and she was expected to meet him for coffee. By the time she had admitted the patient she was even later, and, with her mind still half on that problem and half on the afternoon list, she had scarcely given a thought to the 'new man'.

Alex. That was all she had had, for four years—no surname, no address, no photograph. She'd thought she had started to forget, but at the first glimpse of him her body leapt to life, her pulse thrumming, her senses alert and alive for the first time in years.

The first surge of joy was quickly dampened, both by the memory of his betrayal and the horror of what had followed, leaving her guarded and wary. Why now? she thought. Why not all those years ago when I had something to offer?

She extended her hand mechanically and took his, touching him for the first time in four years, but she had forgotten nothing. His hand was hard and warm, lean, strong, the back scattered with dark hair, but his grip, although firm, was gentle. She felt his touch like a surge of electricity right through to her bones.

He looked older but more relaxed now. The hunted look was gone, but it had left its mark in the lines around his eyes and the touch of grey at his temples. He was heavier, too, his shoulders broader, his chest deeper than before.

She met his eyes, that gentle brown that was so warm, and saw a wealth of remembrance.

'Hello, Alex,' she said, annoyed that her voice was husky and tinged with a distinctly unprofessional intimacy.

Owen Davie glanced from one to the other. 'I take it you've met?'

'Yes—I——'

'We met once, briefly, several years ago in London,' Alex explained smoothly. 'We didn't get as far as surnames.'

Jo extracted her hand from his, and tucked it in her

pocket to disguise the sudden tremor. Was she the only one who could see the mockery lurking in his eyes? Surnames were the only thing they hadn't got around to, she remembered with a vivid clarity that brought a soft touch of colour to her pale skin.

Then Owen's bleep went and he excused himself.

'I'll leave you two to become reacquainted over coffee—perhaps you could allow him to accompany you in Theatre this afternoon, Joanna?'

And he was gone, leaving them alone in the heaving, seething crowd. They might as well have been on a desert island for all the notice they took of the others.

It had been so long—so endlessly, achingly long—since they had met and parted. He studied her face intently, as if he was searching for the secret of eternal youth. She could understand. She couldn't take her eyes off him either, feasting hungrily on the features that were burned into her heart, memorising all the little changes.

After what seemed like an age, she dragged her eyes away and waved at the queue.

'Shall we?'

His mouth softened imperceptibly. You couldn't by any stretch of the imagination call it a smile, but then she'd never seen him smile, so she wasn't surprised.

'Good idea. I had an early start this morning, so I'm ready for it. Can I get you one?'

'I'll have tea.' They joined the queue and she smiled vacantly at her colleagues and turned back to him. 'Where have you come from?'

'Surrey—I've just been tidying up loose ends at my old hospital and handing over to the new senior registrar.'

Her eyes flicked up and met his.

'I thought you were in London?'

'I was—until three years ago. I needed. . .' He hesitated and glanced away. 'I needed a change. How about you? Have you been here long?'

She swallowed. 'Four years.'

His warm brown eyes swept over her and settled gently on her face. 'All that time,' he said softly.

'Tea or coffee, dear?'

'Oh!' She dragged herself back to reality, collected their drinks and allowed Alex to pay for them. The crowd was thinning by this time and she led him to a low table and a group of easy-chairs by the window.

Sparrows were picking at the paving outside, and she watched them absently as she stirred her tea. She was conscious of Alex watching her, his eyes assessing, and she was glad she had worn the smart linen dress today.

'You look very lovely,' he said quietly. 'I'd forgotten just how lovely you are.'

Perversely, because he seemed to have read her mind, she was cross with him. Surely he didn't expect to go straight back and pick up where they had left off?

Her cheeks blushed a soft peach, and she looked away again.

'I'm sorry, I've embarrassed you. OK, no more personal remarks, and I'll do my best not to remember how you felt in my arms, if you could manage to wear something shapeless and put a bag over your head and not look at me with those wide and wicked eyes.'

She gave a surprised laugh, and his mouth softened again.

'That's better. Now, Dr Harding, perhaps you could do your bit to welcome me to the hospital and then when we've got that out of the way I can ask you to have dinner with me tonight.'

She fiddled with her cup. 'I don't think that would be a good idea.'

'To welcome me to the hospital? I'm sure that was what Owen Davie intended——'

'I meant dinner.'

'I haven't asked you yet.'

'I don't think you'd better bother——'

'It would be no bother, Jo, and we do need to talk.'

'There's nothing to talk about.' She set her cup down firmly. 'Look, Alex, what happened four years ago— that night was a one-off. It was totally out of character for me to do something like that——'

'I realise that. It was out of character for me, too.' His mouth quirked briefly into a rueful grin. 'I wasn't suggesting a night of wild passion, Jo—just a quiet get-together to see where we go from here.'

She looked up, startled. 'Why should you imagine that we'll go anywhere? We're going to be colleagues— to be quite brutally specific, you're going to be my boss. That's where we're going, Mr Carter.'

She could hear the bitterness in her voice, but there was nothing she could do about it. She *was* bitter. He was sitting there in his dark suit and his sober tie, looking like a Savile Row fashion plate, in *her* job, in *her* hospital. The hell of it was, she had just got him out of her system, had started to get through the nights without dreaming of him, and now here he was, back in her life, doing all sorts of things to her pulse-rate and threatening her hard-won status quo.

'Is there someone else?' he asked now.

Someone else? After what had happened, after all

those nights reliving the short hours in his arms? 'Not at the moment,' she covered.

'You hadn't forgotten me,' he said quietly.

'Not for want of trying,' she retorted sharply before she could stop herself.

One eyebrow rose. 'I'm flattered that I was so memorable.'

'Don't be,' she snapped. 'I wasn't trying to flatter you. You left my life in chaos——'

He groaned softly. 'I'm sorry. I never meant to hurt you.'

'You left without even saying goodbye!' She tried to keep the hurt out of her voice, but it was there anyway.

His face was expressionless, only his eyes reflecting her anguish.

'I had my reasons,' he said quietly. 'I went back to your flat three weeks later, but you'd gone.'

She nodded. 'I was here.'

'I wanted to know—if there had been any repercussions.'

Her heart jerked with the force of the pain. 'No,' she said numbly. 'No repercussions.' None that was visible to the naked eye, at least.

Her hand slid to her lap and clenched against the taut wall of her abdomen. Trying to act calmly, she got to her feet and picked up her white coat.

'I have to get back to my clinic. Why don't you go up to the ward and make yourself at home? I'll come up there when I've finished my clinic and take you to lunch, and then you can come into Theatre this afternoon with me if you like.'

'Fine.' He stood up, and for a second their eyes met, almost on a level, before she turned away.

'Come on, then, I'll tell you where to go.'

'I thought you already had,' he said softly behind her, and she stifled the chuckle. It wasn't hard. She really had very little to laugh about.

Her clinic took all her concentration. Not that any of the cases were complicated, but she found herself missing the answers to her questions, and collecting a lot of strange looks from her nursing staff as well as the patients.

In the end she excused her behaviour on the grounds of a headache and somehow finished off without any major hiccups.

She was later than she had intended, though, and by the time she reached the ward Alex had been taken to lunch by Owen Davie.

She found them in the staff canteen and he looked up and waved to her immediately, as if he had been looking out for her. She waved back, collected a salad and fruit juice and made her way over to the table, trying to ignore the pounding of her heart.

He stood as she approached and held her chair for her in an entirely natural display of good manners that sat easily with his quiet reticence.

Nevertheless it irritated her, and she flashed him a challenging look that he met with steady confidence.

'Such gallantry!' she quipped lightly, with just the merest touch of acid.

'Such feminist rebellion!' he murmured as he returned to his seat. 'Successful morning?'

'Not bad. Did you see Mary Jenkins, Owen?'

The consultant nodded. 'I did. She's settled into the ward and we'll watch her over the weekend. If her blood-pressure doesn't come down by Monday then I think we'll have to induce her. She's almost at term.' He turned to Alex. 'Of course she'll be your patient then, and it'll be up to you how you deal with it, but I'll leave her notes fully written up for you. I expect to be in and out over the weekend.'

'Can you fill me in?' Alex asked.

Owen shrugged and waved to Jo. 'Your patient.'

She nodded. 'OK. She's twenty-nine, and it's her first visit to us. She's thirty-seven weeks pregnant. Her community midwife saw her in the street, took one look at her face and told her she needed to see the doctor for antenatal treatment. He referred her to us as a matter of urgency yesterday afternoon.

'She's very severely oedematous, and her blood-pressure this morning was 210 over 130. She's also showing signs of severe proteinuria, and generally she's thoroughly pre-eclamptic. However, the ultrasound scan showed the baby to be a good size and moving well, so I didn't think there was any urgency to induce her until her blood-pressure had a chance to come down. I imagine she's been put on a diuretic and a hypotensive——' Owen nodded '—and we'll watch her closely for any deterioration.'

'First baby?' Alex asked.

'Yes. She's unmarried and not the most intelligent person I've ever met. I imagine she thought the bloating was all part of pregnancy.'

She prodded her fork into her salad and moved it round the plate. Alex's hand lay distractingly on the table just on the periphery of her vision, and she could see the fine dark hairs over the prominent bones of his wrist. His fingers were long and supple, the skin soft and smooth in deference to his patients, but the hands themselves were strong, sensitive and very, very clever.

She felt her skin heat and turned her head slightly so that her hair fell forward and screened her face.

'So what's the list this afternoon?' he asked her.

'Gynae,' she replied shortly. 'Three D and Cs, a hysterectomy and a prolapse repair.'

'On a Friday afternoon?' He sounded surprised.

'The D and C patients can go home tomorrow morning and have someone to look after them over the weekend. Otherwise they tend just to get up and carry on, and then they feel lousy. The hysterectomy is an emergency following a very heavy bleed due to fibroids—we've finally got her blood count up enough to tackle it—and the prolapse lady cancelled three months ago and finally had to come back to us because she'd deteriorated so badly she's desperate.'

'Why not leave her till Monday?'

'Because she'll have all weekend to fret and she'll probably run away again. Anyway, we can't do all our operations on a Monday; we have to share Theatre time with the other gynae teams.'

'Do you have a theatre problem?'

'Doesn't everybody these days?' Owen asked drily. 'And anyway, one of the reasons for getting these cases out of the way is to give you the easiest possible lead-in until you're used to the set-up, so don't tell her off for being helpful, there's a good chap.'

Alex shot her an apologetic glance. 'Was I? I'm sorry, I didn't mean to. Are you going to eat that or just shove it round the plate?'

Jo looked down at her mangled salad and sighed.

She really didn't fancy it, but she needed something before she went up to Theatre——

'Can I get you a piece of cake or something? You ought to eat.'

She tried to smile. If it weren't for him she wouldn't have had any trouble eating!

'Thanks—fruit cake would be nice.'

'Coffee?'

'Tea—please. Thanks, Alex.'

She watched him walk away, and then turned back to find Owen regarding her seriously.

'Did you know him—er—very well?'

She grinned ruefully. 'Better than I should have done, and really not at all.'

'I don't understand——'

'Neither did I.'

He shook his head slowly, then raised it again and looked searchingly at her, realisation dawning. 'Was it him?'

'Yes.' She gave a sad little smile. 'Don't worry, Owen, I'll be OK. Just—don't say anything, please?'

'Joanna!'

'Don't be offended. I just can't afford to take the risk that he'll find out.'

The older man covered her hand and squeezed it reassuringly. 'He'll find out nothing from me, my dear. About the job——'

Her smile slipped.

'I want you to know I recommended you for it. I know we haven't always agreed, but I think you'll make a damn fine consultant one day. I'm just sorry that it couldn't be now.'

'Thank you, Owen. I'm glad you told me—you've taught me such a lot in the last four years.'

He grinned reluctantly. 'I've learnt a lot from you, as well. You've been very interesting to work with——'

'That's not what you said about the aromatherapy!'

They laughed, a new warmth between them, and Jo felt a sharp twist of sorrow that her old mentor was moving on to pastures new.

'I'll miss you, you know. It'll be strange without you.'

'Carter'll soon make his mark. I expect you'll see some changes in the next few weeks.'

Jo was sure they would—and most of them in her blood-pressure!

'Her cervix is very elongated so I'm going to do a Manchester repair,' Jo explained to the theatre staff later that afternoon.

The patient was lying on the table with her feet suspended in stirrups, and as she settled herself on the stool ready to begin Jo was very conscious of Alex's presence just behind her shoulder. In theatre boots she lost the advantage of her high heels, and he seemed to tower over her. In fact, of course, he was only about four inches taller than her at most, but, as she herself was five feet ten, she wasn't used to many people being taller.

She had taken a hated disadvantage and turned it into a frank asset as she had matured and forged her career, but, as she swivelled round on the stool and tipped back her head to meet Alex's eyes far above her, she was suddenly all the more aware of how big he was. He made her feel small and dainty and—dear God, now was not the time to think of how he made her feel!

It was a tricky repair and required all her concentration, and gradually she forgot about Alex's presence behind her and focused on her patient.

At one point the heat of the theatre was almost overwhelming, and she could feel the moisture pooling in droplets on her brow and in the cleft between her breasts.

Before she could speak Alex's hand appeared and swabbed her brow.

'Better?' he murmured, and she nodded.

'Thank you. Right, I just want to attach these ligaments here and I can close her up. Can I have some sutures, please?'

As they left the operating theatre a short while later, he said quietly for her ears only, 'Well done. That was a tricky one—you did it very neatly. I don't think I could have done it better myself.'

She was warmed and yet irritated by his words of praise, and he was quick to pick up on it.

'Have I patronised you?'

She gave a reluctant laugh. 'Only a tiny bit.'

He smiled slightly. 'About tonight——'

'I can't—even if I wanted to, I've promised to babysit for Anne Gabriel.'

'I could bring a take-away and join you.'

'I——'

For the life of her she couldn't think of a single reason why he couldn't, but all her senses were screaming 'No!'. All except her treacherous heart.

'You'll have the children to chaperon you,' he said reasonably.

'Child. Beth. She's six and a half.'

He waited patiently, while all the theatre staff milled around them, and she chewed her lip and doubted the intelligence she was born with.

'I'm vegetarian,' she warned him.

He shrugged. 'I can live with that.'

Her heart thumped at the thought of living with this disturbing man.

'OK. Meet me there at eight.' She scribbled the address on a pad and ripped off the sheet. 'Here. It's easy to find—Reception will direct you; they're hospital houses.'

'Chinese or Indian?'

'Either. I must go.'

He nodded. 'I'll see you later.'

As she went through to Recovery to check on her patients, she thought she must finally have lost her marbles.

Beth met her at the door, a bright-eyed, lively little girl with coltish limbs and a delicate face surrounded by thick dark brown tresses.

'Hi, Auntie Jo!'

'Hi, sweetheart. Is Mummy ready yet?'

'Nearly. Come and see what I did at my babysitter's today!'

Jo allowed herself to be dragged into the dingy little sitting-room at the back of the house and sat on the old sofa while Beth proudly showed her a mutilated piece of paper with coloured splodges on it. Stuck to the splodges were lumps of raw pasta.

'It's a pasta picture,' Beth told her unnecessarily.

'I can see that,' Jo said. 'Tell me about it.'

'It's meant to be ducks in the park. Mummy said it looked like a fight in an Italian restaurant. Sometimes she's mean.'

Jo suppressed the urge to laugh. 'I'm sure she was only teasing you, darling.'

Beth's lip wobbled. 'I didn't want to be teased,' she said unsteadily.

Jo sighed and ruffled Beth's soft hair. 'She didn't mean to upset you, treasure. I think she's very tired, Beth, and just needs time to herself sometimes. She works awfully hard, you know, darling.'

'I know.' Beth's little face was resigned. 'Can I have a cuddle, Auntie Jo?'

Jo hugged her quickly. 'In a minute. I just want to tell Mummy something. Why don't you find a nice book for me to read you?'

Leaving the child sorting through the bookcase in the sitting-room, Jo ran lightly up the stairs and tapped on the door of the larger bedroom.

'Come in!'

She pushed open the door and went in, sighing at the chaos. Anne was sitting at the dressing-table, carefully concealing the dark shadows under her eyes. Clothes were strewn all over the bed.

'Heavy date?' she asked with irony.

'Oh, don't! I don't know what to say to him, Jo. I wish he hadn't proposed—I was just getting all ready to end it and he went and popped the question!'

'He' was Colin Bradley, a charming and delightful solicitor, widowed, with two young daughters a little older than Beth, and his interest in Anne was so blatantly as a mother substitute that they had found his declaration of love almost laughable. Laughable, that was, until Anne had realised that he meant it.

'He's a dear man, but——' Anne shuddered slightly. 'Jo, I could never sleep with him! Not after. . . I just couldn't.'

Jo shoved the clothes out of the way and sat on the end of the bed.

'Are you quite sure you've considered all the benefits of marriage to him sufficiently? OK, so you don't find him all that attractive, but there's not that much wrong with him, and he'd be a good father to Beth. And God knows you could do with a little company. Is having to sleep with him such a huge price to pay?'

Anne turned to face her friend. 'I've known you for twelve years, Jo. Could you do it?'

Jo thought of Alex, of the searing ecstasy of that one night in his arms, and then thought of spending the rest of her life going through a pale imitation of that night with another man.

'No—no, I couldn't,' she said softly. 'You're right— and both you and Beth deserve far more than that. I think Colin does, too. Yes, you're right—tell him this evening.'

Anne sighed. 'He'll be here in a minute. Oh, life's always so complicated!'

Jo thought again of Alex.

'Annie, I have a confession. Someone's coming round to keep me company this evening. I hope you don't mind.'

Her friend paused in the act of hanging up the clothes again. 'A man?'

Jo nodded.

'Great—about time. Anyone I know?'

She nodded again. 'Our new consultant.'

Anne whistled. 'Blimey, that was quick!'

'Not really. Our last date was four years ago.'

Anne dropped the dress she was holding, and stared at Jo in horror. 'What. . .?'

Jo nodded slowly.

'My God. And I thought I had problems.'

CHAPTER TWO

BY EIGHT o'clock, Jo's nerves were stretched tighter than a bow-string. Anne had gone with Colin, her nerves nearly as taut, and Beth, intuitive as always, had picked up on the tension and had been unusually awkward about going to bed.

Now, at almost exactly eight o'clock, Jo was alone. Beth was finally asleep, the sitting-room was still dingy but the toys were put away and the cushions patted into shape, and she had washed up Beth's supper dishes and tidied the kitchen.

There were plates warming, the rickety table in the kitchen was laid, and there was nothing left to do but count her remaining marbles and wonder what on earth she'd let herself in for.

She hadn't changed—apart from anything else she didn't want him to think she was making an effort to impress him, and dressing down wouldn't have fooled him either. So she was still in the dark green linen dress with the red belt and the high-heeled shoes to match. Her feet ached, but after the events of the day she was unwilling to lose even the slight advantage of height to him.

At eight o'clock precisely a big Rover pulled up smoothly outside and Alex got out and locked it. Jo stood at the kitchen window and watched as he walked towards the door, his easy stride bringing him closer with horrifying speed.

He saw her and lifted his hand, and she walked slowly out into the hall, her heart pounding. Closing her eyes, she drew a deep, calming breath and then opened the door.

He looked wonderful. He had abandoned the suit jacket and tie, and was wearing a soft blue cotton sweater over his shirt. One side of his mouth almost smiled, and her own mouth curved in response.

'Aren't you going to ask me in?' he teased softly.

She flushed. 'I'm sorry—of course—come in.' Whatever was the matter with her? She was behaving like a lovesick teenager!

She led the way into the kitchen and he put the bag he was holding on the worktop.

'I got Indian—mainly because it was the first take-away I found. Is that OK?'

'Fine. I'm starving.'

'Me too. It was a long time ago that you didn't eat your lunch.'

She laughed, a deep, husky chuckle that relieved the tension in the air between them.

They dished up the meal and ate it ravenously, and when they had finished Jo pushed away her plate with a satisfied groan.

'Wow!'

Alex's eyes flickered briefly over her and returned to her face.

'My sentiments exactly.'

Which brought the tension slamming back and clogged the breath in her throat and pooled the heat low down in her body. She stood up abruptly and made her trembling legs take her over to the sink. Perhaps she should have dressed down—to the shapeless garments he had talked about earlier?

'Coffee?' she asked over her shoulder.

'Thank you, that would be lovely.'

She ran the water into the kettle, plugged it in and reached up to get down the coffee.

She hadn't heard him move but he must have done, because suddenly his hand closed over hers and he turned her gently into his arms.

'Jo,' he whispered against her hair, and her traitorous body sagged against him, revelling in the sleek hardness of his legs, the solid depth of his chest, the shift of warm supple muscles beneath her palms as her hands crept round his waist and came to rest each side of his spine.

She had kicked off her shoes under the table and her eyes were on a level with his mouth. She could see the dark shadow on his jaw, and the slight sheen of his skin where he had just recently shaved. His lips were full and firm, and any second——

'Alex, no,' she moaned softly as his mouth closed over hers with infinite gentleness.

He withdrew fractionally, but only to run his tongue lightly over the edge of her lips, then he drew the lower lip into his mouth and nibbled with tiny biting kisses, easing away again to soothe it with his tongue.

Jo started to shake, her hands winding up around his neck to pull his head down, and then the kiss spiralled out of control and they clung to each other as the passion mounted in them, driving them with its frenzied zeal.

She twisted against him and with a groan he pressed her back against the cupboards, imprinting his body on hers with a wild savagery that made her whimper with need.

Eventually they broke apart, gasping for breath, and in his eyes Jo could see white-hot desire tinged with remorse.

'Dear God, Alex,' she whispered, shaken by the depth of her response. 'Why did you have to do that?'

'I'm sorry,' he said raggedly, 'but it's been so damn long. . .'

He let her go and she sagged back against the worktop, her legs like jelly.

He turned away, and she noticed his breathing was still uneven. He was also still unmistakably aroused, and she had to grip the worktop hard to stop herself from running across the kitchen after him and throwing herself into his arms.

'Why don't you wait in the sitting-room and I'll bring the coffee through in a minute?' she suggested unsteadily, and with a brief nod he complied.

Once alone, she dropped her face into her hands and stood motionless for a moment, willing her unruly body to submit to discipline. Then she gathered up the wreckage of their meal, threw it in the dustbin, put the plates in hot soapy water and scrubbed down the table before turning her attention back to the coffee.

By the time she took it through to the little sitting-room, Alex was sitting in one of the chairs with one leg crossed over the other knee and his hands lying relaxed along the threadbare arms.

He watched her thoughtfully, and she avoided his eye, unable to look at him for fear of betraying herself.

She set his cup down beside him and retreated to the other chair, drawing up her long legs and curling them

underneath her defensively. She knew she was doing
it, but she also knew that if she didn't sit on her feet
the wretched things were quite likely to carry her over
and dump her in his lap, and she couldn't afford that
sort of complication.

She nursed her cup of tea and waited for him to
speak. After a few minutes of tortured silence, he
heaved a sigh and picked up his coffee.

'I'm sorry,' he said heavily. 'I didn't mean that to
happen. I really just wanted to talk to you about the
last four years—find out how you were, what you'd
been doing, if you were married yet—all that sort of
thing. I certainly didn't mean to fall on you like a sex-
starved teenager and grope you at the first
opportunity.'

She laughed reluctantly. 'I wasn't aware that you did
grope me.'

'Thank God for little miracles,' he said drily,
'because I certainly wanted to.'

She met his eyes then, and saw regret and a gentle
tenderness there that nearly undid her resolve.

She looked quickly away.

'Alex, I'm not interested,' she said as firmly as she
could manage. 'I've got my career all mapped out, and
I know exactly where I'm going. OK, I didn't get this
job, but I'll get the next one that comes along, or the
one after that—I'm determined to succeed, and I can't
afford the luxury of anything that could get in the way
of that ambition.'

He was watching her, and she kept her eyes averted
in case he read the miserable truth.

'That doesn't sound like you,' he said at last. 'OK,
you dress the part, and you act the part to a certain

extent, and I don't doubt that you're a damn fine doctor, but there's more to you than that, Jo. You're lonely, and, whatever you might say to the contrary, you're interested. At least be honest with me.'

Oh, God, she thought, honest is the last thing I can be with you. She fought off the wave of sadness and made herself meet his eye.

'All right, Alex, I'll be honest with you,' she lied. 'Yes, I'm interested—physically. Sexually we're great together, and I'm interested in you as a person. That doesn't mean that I want to try and establish a relationship with you—especially not one that's going to interfere with my career progression. And yes, I'm lonely, but it's what I've chosen, Alex. Look at me!' She spread her arms wide. 'I know how I look—I'm not a fool. If I wanted a man I could have one, but I don't. If you weren't my boss, then I dare say we could have a great affair, but as things stand it's out of the question, and, the sooner you realise that, the better for both of us.'

He was silent for a long while, and she risked a quick glance at him. His mouth was tight, his chin propped on his steepled fingers, and his eyes as they met hers were cold. She realised she had hurt him with her deliberately crude and harsh assessment of their relationship, and somehow that was worse than any-thing else. Then he rose to his feet and walked over to the window. His hands were rammed in his pockets and the tension was pouring off him.

'So that's it, is it? Your final word?'

'That's right. It's the way it has to be, Alex. I'm sorry.'

He snorted. 'Spare me the platitudes.' He swivelled round to face her, his eyes hard and unyielding.

'Either you're lying, or you really are a hard-bitten career doctor with a hyperactive sex drive. Either way, you're not the woman I thought you were.'

Shock held her rigid. She stared at the spot where his feet had been, and listened as he walked down the hall and let himself quietly out of the front door.

So that was the end of that. At least she had stopped him in his tracks, but it hurt her that she had had to lose his respect in order to do so.

Jo got wearily to her feet and cleared away the cups, then washed the dishes in the sink and tidied up the kitchen.

She was just putting the last few things away when Anne came home.

'Hi,' she said with forced cheer. 'Thanks for tidying up—how's Beth been?'

'Fine—how did it go?'

Jo took one look at her friend's ravaged face and held out her arms.

'Oh, Annie. . .'

Anne collapsed into her arms and sobbed out her misery while Jo soothed and patted and held her until she was finished, then she handed her a wodge of tissues and steered her to the kitchen table.

'Tell,' she said firmly.

'Oh, he was very upset, and I cried, and it was awful, but I couldn't have married him. It wouldn't have been fair, and I think he saw that in the end.' She sniffed and blew her nose. 'He wants us to be friends. I said no. Do you think that was too unkind?'

'No.' Jo shook her head emphatically. 'No, you can't

be friends when one of you's in love and the other isn't. It would be a disaster for both of you.'

Anne sighed. 'That's what I thought, but I still felt awful saying it. So, how about you? How did you get on with Alex? Did he make a pass at you?'

Jo flushed and looked away. 'Not exactly, but he made it quite clear he'd be happy to take up where we left off.'

Anne chewed her lip thoughtfully, then covered Jo's hand with her own.

'Why don't you tell him?'

Jo snatched her hand away and stood up. 'No—I—I can't! He'll only feel guilty, and it isn't his fault——'

'Any more than it's yours.'

'It's my body!'

'That doesn't make it your fault. Are you using it as an excuse?'

'For what? Not sleeping with him again? We're talking about sex here, Anne!'

Her friend regarded her steadily. 'Are we? It strikes me you've never got over him.'

'Damn it, Annie, there was nothing to get over—one night!'

Anne's face twisted with pain. 'A great deal can happen in one night,' she said quietly, 'as you well know.'

Jo sagged against the table. 'OK, OK, I never really got over him. But for him it's just sex——'

'Are you sure?'

Jo stood up impatiently and strode across the room. 'Don't be silly! He's a man—men feel differently about these things. Anyway, it's not a problem any more. I told him I was a career doctor——'

'You?'

She glared at Anne. 'Yes, me! Don't laugh. Anyway, he wasn't impressed. He told me I wasn't the woman he thought I was, and walked out. I think I dented his ego, and fair's fair—he dented mine.'

'Are you angry with him about getting the job?'

She shrugged. 'A bit. He watched me operate this afternoon and told me he couldn't have done it better himself. As that was just what I've been trying to tell people, it was really the last thing I wanted to hear!'

Anne chuckled. 'He's going to have to watch himself around you, isn't he? Poor man won't be able to breathe without being snapped at.'

'I'm sure the poor man will cope,' she said bitterly.

'You really do hate him, don't you?'

Jo's mouth trembled and she bit her lip. 'No, I don't hate him. All I'm asking is to be left alone.' She picked up her bag, slipped on her shoes and headed for the door.

'See you on Monday,' she said heavily, and let herself out.

The drive home was short but she found it hard to concentrate. She kept seeing Alex's face, and hearing his voice telling her she wasn't the person he thought she was.

She turned into her little drive and locked her car, then let herself into the tiny semi-detached cottage that had been her home for three and a half years.

She locked up and headed straight for the stairs. She couldn't be bothered to make herself a hot drink tonight. All she wanted was the oblivion of sleep, but it wouldn't come.

She lay on her back in the bed and her hands slid

slowly down the smooth, taut line of her abdomen and over the hollow of her pelvis.

There, running from side to side in the crease above her pubic bone, and almost hidden by the dense tangle of soft auburn curls, was the faint ridge of the scar.

It had faded in four years, but it would never go, and it would take a gynaecologist all of two seconds to assess the possible significance and start asking questions.

He must never get that close to her, and the only way she could ensure that he didn't was to keep him severely at a distance. It seemed likely that she had achieved that aim particularly effectively, she thought with bitter irony.

But her body ached for him, and with a muffled groan she turned her face into the pillow and allowed her imagination to run riot.

Monday came far too soon. He was on the ward already when she arrived at eight, and she found him in Mary Jenkins' room studying her charts.

He glanced up, said, 'Good morning,' under his breath, and continued to study the charts.

After a few seconds he returned the board to the end of her bed and left the room, beckoning Jo to follow.

'She's worse,' he said briefly. 'She'll have to have a section now. Her BP's still climbing, and the hydralla-zine isn't touching it. She's not losing fluid significantly, either, and she complained of a headache this morning. I don't think we can leave it, and, frankly, I'm not happy to induce her. I popped in last night with Owen Davie and we decided that the night staff should watch her and, if she deteriorated, they should assume she's going to Theatre this morning, so she's had nothing by mouth since midnight and she had her premed an hour ago when I came in.'

'Has she signed the consent form?'

He nodded. 'The paperwork's been done.' He met her eyes, his face carefully blank.

'Your theatre's all ready—we'll use that. Your list will be delayed a while, I'm afraid, but it can't be helped.'

Jo tried to control her anger. It was her list that day—and Mary Jenkins had been admitted by her. She should be in charge, but Alex was obviously making a point by taking over.

'It could get tricky,' he said softly. 'Would you mind if I assist?'

So she was to perform the operation after all! He could easily have taken over, but he hadn't, and she felt her resentment simply drain away.

'Of course not,' she said quietly. 'Are you going up now?'

He nodded.

'I have a couple of patients for my list later this morning I'd like to see first, if I've got time?'

'Fine. I'll see you up there.'

He hesitated, as if he was going to say something else, and then turned away abruptly. She watched him go with mixed feelings, and then went through into the four-bedded ward where her two pre-op patients for that morning were waiting.

The first lady, June Turner, was in for a routine Caesarean section, her fourth in six years.

Jo perched on the end of her bed and smiled.

'Hello, June. How are you?'

'Marvellous! Mike's coming in soon ready for the big event—oh, here he is now! Hello, darling!'

The stocky young man bent and kissed his wife, and smiled confidently at Jo. 'Morning, Dr Harding. All ready for off?'

'Yes, she's all ready, but we may have a minor delay. I'm glad you're here, though, because I wanted to talk to you again about sterilisation——'

'No!' they said in unison.

Jo sighed. 'You know, having so many pregnancies with a scarred uterus is just asking for trouble; you've got three lovely children, and this baby—don't you think you're being just a little rash?'

June smiled. 'Why don't you let us worry about that? We know the risks—we're intelligent and educated, and we've talked about it at great length. Don't worry, Dr Harding, we don't intend to have any more, but neither of us is happy with the idea of losing our choice. We won't have an accident.'

Jo laughed. 'How many times have I heard that? OK, I'll leave it for now, but I thought I'd just check to see if you'd changed your minds before we take you up to Theatre. When I see the scar and how it's standing up, I'll discuss it with you at the time. You don't have to decide now.' She stood up. 'I'll see you both later.'

With a smile, she left the Turners and moved on to the next room.

The woman lying there was very still, and Jo sat beside her and watched her for a second before touching her hand.

'Mrs Price? Sally?'

The woman turned her head towards Jo and smiled wearily. 'Hi.'

'How are you feeling?'

She shrugged. 'I'm just wondering if there's any point. I'm bound to lose it anyway, and in the circumstances perhaps it would be the best thing——'

She turned away, and Jo squeezed her hand.

'Be positive, Sally. Your husband wouldn't want to see you so sad.'

'We've tried for so long—so many miscarriages. For him to die now, when I've got to this stage——'

Jo felt helpless as she watched the woman's shoulders shaking gently with grief. She had been widowed in a senseless accident two months before, and was in to have a cervical suture put in to try and prevent the loss of this most precious baby, the last in a long line of tragic attempts to carry a baby to term.

Owen had refused to give her a cervical suture with the last, maintaining that there was little chance of it working anyway and she was young, so there was plenty of time, but this time was quite literally her last chance to have her husband's child, and Jo had fought tooth and nail. In the end Owen had agreed.

'I'm sorry,' Mrs Price said quietly now. 'I know I'll feel differently about it later, but it's just that I can't bear the thought of any more pain—you know, it's a real bereavement. I didn't realise until Tony died that I had felt the same way every time I lost a baby. Each time you build up such hope, and each time—it's just too much, after a while. I almost wish it would just happen and then it would be over.'

Jo was more determined than ever that this woman would carry her baby to term and know the joy of motherhood.

She stood up. 'One day at a time, Sally,' she told her

gently. 'I'll see you this afternoon to tell you how it went.'

Donning her confident, professional smile, Jo swept out of the ward and up to Theatre. There, in the changing-room, she leant against the cubicle wall and emptied her mind. Deep in the background was the sadness, but that never truly left her, and was a spur and motivation for the way she lived her life. Now, she had to make sure that Mary Jenkins' baby survived her mother's illness and was safely delivered.

Scrubbed and changed into the disgustingly unflattering green theatre pyjamas and white anti-static boots, her gown and mask tied, she made her way into the operating theatre where Alex was already waiting.

Their patient was in the ante-room, and Jo could hear the anaesthetist talking to her.

Suddenly he stuck his head round the corner.

'She's complaining of flashing lights—I think she could be going into a fit.'

Jo moved instantly, but Alex was there before her, snapping out orders and setting up a lytic cocktail drip which was attached to the cannula mercifully already in her arm.

As he connected it, she went into the tonic stage of the convulsion, her body going rigid, her face contorted. After a few seconds she lapsed into the clonic stage, jerking uncontrollably. They held her arm still to try and prevent the drip from being wrenched out, and gradually as the sedatives took effect the convulsions eased and she lapsed into a coma.

Jo looked up and met Alex's eyes, and he winked at her reassuringly.

'Your patient, Dr Harding—I think we should proceed with the section when we've scrubbed again.'

She smiled faintly at him. 'Good idea.'

They walked out to the scrub-room and stood side by side at the sinks. She was tempted to lean on him, and tell him how grateful she was that he had been there to share the horror of that moment.

She'd never seen an eclamptic fit before, and, while she was glad that better antenatal care had removed the risk almost completely, she had to admit that it did nothing to prepare you for an unexpected case like Mary Jenkins.

She dried her hands, pulled on a fresh set of gloves and made her way back with Alex into the operating-room.

Their patient was on the table, draped and swabbed and ready for her attention.

Alex stood quietly opposite her, his hands ready to cauterise or irrigate or hold retractors, always steady, there before she had to ask, but never once commenting or implying that he would have done it differently.

Finally she was through all the layers of muscle and into the uterus, and as he held the retractors steady, she reached inside and brought out a tiny, squalling scrap.

There was a collective sigh of relief as the baby yelled her protest, and Alex smiled at her.

Jo looked away. 'She looks fine,' she said abruptly, and clamped the cord and cut it.

The midwife took the baby to a cot and laid her in, and checked her Apgar score while Jo delivered the placenta and started suturing.

'Apgar nine,' the midwife said after five minutes, and Jo nodded.

'Lucky,' Alex commented.

'Thanks to your quick action,' Jo said, echoing all their feelings. There was a general murmur of agreement.

At last she had tied the final suture and the woman was wheeled away to Recovery.

Alex and Jo went up to the little rest-room and relaxed while the theatre was prepared for the next case.

'You were very generous,' he said, 'especially considering that I took over your patient.'

She smiled. 'I didn't mind,' she assured him. 'I was just grateful for your quick action.'

'I only did what you would have done.'

She shrugged. 'Maybe.'

He looked steadily at her. 'You would have coped.'

'I know, but I'm still glad you were there.'

He looked quickly away. 'Tell me about your list,' he instructed.

She filled him in, and he nodded but didn't comment, except to ask if she minded if he watched.

'Of course not,' she replied, but her heart thudded, either with tension because he would be watching again or delight because he would still be near her. If she was honest, it was probably both.

The first patient on the list proper was June Turner, who by now had had her epidural set up and was waiting for them in Theatre, her gowned and masked husband waiting at her side.

'Hello, June; hello, Mike,' Jo said cheerfully. 'I'm

sorry to keep you waiting—we had a bit of an emergency. This is Alexander Carter, the new consultant.'

June's relaxed smile faded a little, and her eyes
flicked from Jo's face to his and back again.

'Oh. Does that mean you aren't going to do the
operation?'

Jo grinned. 'No way. I'm not handing you over to
anyone! Right, are you all set?'

The green screens were set up, masking their activity
from June and her husband, and she was swabbed and
draped ready for her operation.

'OK, June, I'm just going to make the first incision
now.'

She stroked lightly and swiftly with the scalpel, and
Anne Gabriel, who was assisting, swabbed and irri-
gated and held retractors and smiled at June over the
curtain as Jo worked.

Jo herself was busy working her way through the
layers of scar tissue in the old incision line. In very
little time she reached the uterus, and looked at June.
'OK, here we are. The scar actually looks fine, so I
suppose that means you don't want to be sterilised?'

Mike grinned. 'Nice try, Dr Harding.'

She laughed. 'OK, I'm just going to open the uterus
and then you'll have your baby.'

June smiled, Mike held her hand even tighter and Jo
carefully penetrated the first layer.

'Suction, please,' she said, but Anne was there
already, and in no time the baby was in her hands. 'It's
a boy,' she said with a smile that lit up her eyes above
her mask, 'and he looks lovely!'

She handed the baby over the screen and into his

mother's waiting arms, and then clamped the cord and cut it as Mike leant over and kissed his son.

The pain crashed into her with all the force of an express train, and she took a steadying breath.

You really would think it would get easier, she mused, but it doesn't, and for some reason today it's even worse. In the midst of all the chaos and congratulations, she lifted her head and met Alex's eyes, and looked away.

Her own must have reflected her misery because later, after the Turner family had left the theatre and Jo had completed her list, she found Alex by her side, his face concerned.

'Are you OK?' he said in an undertone.

'Of course I'm OK. Why should I not be?'

He shrugged. 'Search me. I just thought you looked a bit pole-axed in there for a minute with the Turners.'

She busied herself removing her soiled gown and putting it in the bin. 'Don't be silly. Everybody's moved by the birth of a baby.'

He moved round in front of her and tipped her chin. 'I didn't say moved, I said——'

'I heard you. You were mistaken. Excuse me.'

She pushed past him and went to shower and change. When she emerged he was gone, and she managed to avoid him for the rest of the day.

She went home exhausted at seven, and made herself an omelette. She was too tired and stressed out to eat it, though, and poked it around for a few minutes before giving up.

Anne rang her later to ask if she was all right.

'Of course I'm all right—what's the matter with you all?' she snapped, and then felt immediately guilty.

Anne, however, knew her too well to take umbrage, and quietly wished her goodnight before hanging up.

It was a long week, and by the end of it Jo's nerves were flayed to a shred.

Alex had been everywhere, popping up like a jack-in-a-box every time she turned round. However, he had taken her at her word and was leaving her alone, making no further attempt to persuade her to go out with him.

He had made a real impact with the staff, and Anne thought he was charming and could quite see why Jo had fallen so hard and so fast.

'Why don't you talk to him?' she said again, and Jo had to avoid her after that.

That afternoon Jo had delivered a baby and Alex had popped in just in time to see her cradling the babe against her breast and holding the tiny hand in her own.

'It suits you—you ought to try it some time,' he suggested, and with a wicked wink he left her.

Anne Gabriel had been there, too, and after one look at Jo's shocked face had taken the baby from her and finished clearing up after the delivery without asking any questions.

As soon as possible, Jo had escaped home and attacked the housework, but that just made her even more exhausted and left her mind whirling in a body that ached from end to end. Feeling even more miserable, she made a cup of tea and took it up to wallow in the bath with a book she hadn't had time to finish.

She undressed and hung up her skirt, throwing the blouse and underwear into the laundry basket.

How could she get Alex Carter out of her mind? He

was haunting her, the might-have-beens overwhelming in the light of his constant presence.

And the worst of it was she still loved him—loved him more with each minute that passed, because she was getting to know him now and everything that she discovered just reinforced her first impressions.

The sadness that she always carried with her seemed almost too heavy to bear tonight. How right he had been, because she *wasn't* the person he had known four years ago. It would be strange if all the things that had happened had left her quite untouched.

She closed the wardrobe door and stood back to study herself with a critical eye.

Her hair was thick and heavy, falling over her shoulders and framing her face with a tumble of wild flame. Her skin was pale and smooth, though cursed with freckles, and her full breasts were firm and creamy, tipped with rose-pink nipples. Below them her waist was neat, her tummy smooth and flat.

Beneath the gentle swell of her hips her legs were endless, long and shapely, and at their juncture the soft, thick curls clustered enticingly.

She was all woman—strong, healthy, designed to tempt a man and lure him to her bed, and there to conceive his children in the wild ecstasy of passion.

Her mouth twisted and her gaze returned to the curls that hid the hated scar.

It was just an illusion, that mother-earth look of hers. She wasn't a woman at all, just a cardboard cut-out, an android, an imposter.

How could you be a woman without a womb?

CHAPTER THREE

FOR most of the people there it was just another party, but Jo was celebrating the end of her last day as an SHO prior to her forthcoming appointment at the Audley Memorial Hospital in Suffolk as a very junior registrar.

Her new boss, Owen Davie, was probably one of the old school, but Jo was confident that she would get a good grounding in what was quite definitely an up and coming hospital.

The long and gruelling year as SHO was finally ended, she had a new job to look forward to, and she was in the mood to party.

Although she was on her own, she wasn't truly on her own. The hospital community was a close-knit one, and she would know most of the people who would be there tonight.

She had dressed with her usual flamboyant zeal, in a silky, figure-hugging sheath with a thigh-high split and a low back, in shimmering coral-pink silk that draped like a dream. With her red hair it should have been a disaster, but it was a devastating combination and she felt as good as she looked.

By the time she arrived the party was already going with a swing, and she found herself a drink and a convivial group of friends and settled down to celebrate.

An hour and a couple of glasses of cheap wine later,

she was dancing with a bespectacled and rather amorous young doctor who was barely tall enough to look her in the eye when the door opened to admit another group of people.

She noticed him immediately, something about him setting him apart from the group and attracting her attention with all the force of a powerful magnet.

He was tall, taller even than her, and thin, his clothes rather loose as if he had lost weight recently or had been ill.

Then he turned, and she was so shaken by the look of utter desolation in his eyes that her steps faltered and she stood quite still, her eyes locked with his.

Her escort floundered to a halt and peered closely at her, asking if she was all right, but she excused herself absently and made her way across the room, elbowing her way through the crowd until she was by his side.

'Hi!' she yelled over the throbbing beat. 'You're a stranger—welcome to the local madhouse. I'm Jo.'

She held out her hand, and after a second he took it and held it, his eyes meshed with hers again. Once again she was struck by the depth of pain in his soft brown eyes.

'My name's Alex,' he said eventually, his voice deep and slightly husky, as if he hadn't used it much recently.

He was still holding her hand, as if he was almost afraid to let her go, and for a second it crossed her mind that he might be crazy. He lifted his other hand and touched her cheek lightly, his fingers cold.

'Are you real?' he murmured. 'You look so lovely— so vibrant and alive. I'd forgotten people could look like that.'

She laughed, a deep, throaty chuckle that triggered

a convulsive movement of his jaw, almost as if it hurt
him to hear her laugh. She realised he wasn't crazy,
just terribly, inexpressibly sad.

'Oh, I'm real,' she said wryly. 'I'm celebrating—
would you like to help me?'

'I'm not sure I'm much use,' he told her with a
helpless shrug, but he kept hold of her hand.

Someone decided it was time to change the tempo,
and the lively music faded out, to be replaced by
Roberta Flack singing 'The First Time Ever I Saw Your
Face'.

'Dance with me,' Jo murmured, and he looked
startled for a moment, as if she had suggested they
should fly.

Then, releasing her hand, he drew her close into the
circle of his arms and rested his forehead against hers.
As they swayed together to the hauntingly beautiful
melody, Jo felt the tension drain out of him and a new,
more vibrant tension replace it, a tension that caught
her up and drew her closer to him, so that she leant
into his body and gave herself up to the sensation.

Her hands were laid against his chest, and she could
feel the unsteady thud of his heart beneath her palms.
Sliding her arms round under his jacket, she eased
nearer to him, and his hands pressed warmly now
against her back, to cradle her closer to his chest. A
small sound, half-groan, half-sigh, escaped him as the
soft fullness of her breasts pressed against the solid
wall of his chest.

'God, you feel so good,' he murmured, and his voice
slurred slightly as if he was a little drunk.

Jo didn't care—who was she to complain? She

snuggled closer and hugged him. 'You feel pretty good yourself,' she said huskily.

She tipped back her head slightly and met his eyes. They were blazing, like a wildfire out of control, and she felt the heat licking at her, drawing her in.

'Let's get out of here,' he rasped, and with a surprisingly strong grip he led her out of the room. 'Where can we go?' he asked, his voice harsh with desperation.

'My flat,' she told him, a trifle breathless. 'Wait here, I'll get my things.'

She ran up the stairs to the flat above and retrieved her jacket and bag, and went back down again.

He was watching her, his eyes riveted by the flash of thigh as she ran down the stairs, and she threw him a laughing glance and held out her hand.

'Come on,' she said, but he took her jacket and helped her into it, with totally unselfconscious bred-in-the-bone good manners. Then he held the door for her, and once they were out in the darkness of the night he wrapped his arm around her shoulders and held her close against his side as they walked quickly round the corner to where he had parked the car.

She slipped her arm around his waist under his jacket, revelling in the warmth of his skin through the fine cotton of his shirt. She could feel the hard jut of his hipbone against hers as they walked, and beneath her arm she could feel the rise and fall of his ribs in time with his rapid breathing.

The drive was accomplished in a tense and nerve-racking silence broken only by her rather distracted directions, and when they arrived she led him up the stairs to her flat, her heart in her mouth.

'Home sweet home,' she said, opening the door with

a flourish and turning on the bare overhead light. She
kicked off her shoes—a thing she never, ever did unless
she was alone—and turned on the desk light, angling it
in to the wall and killing the harsh glare of the overhead
bulb with a flick of the switch.

'*Voilà*—ambience!'

He gave a dry chuckle, and Jo sighed and looked
round the flat with a disparaging shrug.

'Not much, is it? Still, it's done me—handy for the
hospital, and I won't be here much longer.'

A flicker of something—relief?—crossed his lean,
aristocratic features.

He didn't ask where she was going—perhaps that
should have warned her, but it didn't.

Instead he leaned back against the sofa and watched
her as she took off her jacket and hung it over a chair.

Then it hit her that she was alone in her flat with a
man about whom she knew absolutely nothing, and
that they were going to make love, and she felt
suddenly shy and awkward. Good grief, she thought,
he hasn't even kissed me and I'm going to let him touch
me in the most intimate way there is! I must be mad. . .

Her previous very few affairs had been with men
she'd known for some considerable time and who were
also friends. This man didn't fit the mould, and she was
quite out of her depth. Perhaps she had misread him.
She didn't think so, though.

'I'd love a coffee,' he suggested, and watched her as
she walked gratefully through the kitchen doorway and
put the kettle on.

'What do you do?' he asked her.

'I'm a doctor,' she replied, still disgustingly proud

now that she was finally registered and actually entitled to the title! 'What about you?'

'Snap—wouldn't you know, at that party?'

She laughed and brought the coffee through on a chipped enamel tray.

'How do you take it?'

'Black, strong, no sugar——'

'Good. So do I. Here. Cheers, Alex!'

His mouth relaxed—it didn't smile, precisely, but she got the feeling he didn't have all that much to smile about. She also got the feeling he was as nervous as her, and suddenly she felt much more at ease.

'Thanks—cheers.'

He drank his coffee, watching her over the rim of the mug, and she watched him back and wondered what it was that had put the anguish in his eyes.

Finally he put his mug down and reached out his hand tentatively, stroking his knuckles gently down her cheek.

'You're beautiful, Jo,' he murmured huskily. 'I want to make love to you.'

Now was the time to say no, to send him away. She knew instinctively he would go if she asked him to. But she wouldn't.

Her heart leaping and crashing against her ribs, she put her mug down, stood up and held her hand out to him.

He took it and rose to his feet, staring down at her for a long moment before following her into the bedroom.

She left the door open, and in the diffused light from the living-room she slowly stripped off her dress and stood in front of him clad only in a scrap of lace and silk that passed as underwear.

His breath caught in his throat, and with a strangled groan he closed his eyes.

'I think I'm dreaming,' he muttered.

'And I'm the Queen of Sheba,' she said with a low laugh, stripping off his tie and easing his jacket down his arms. He was trembling, but so was she. His shirt buttons were too difficult and he had to help her, but even he despaired and tore off the last two in his haste to be rid of the shirt.

Then he folded her into his arms and sighed with contentment.

'What on earth is this little bit of nothing?' he asked raggedly, flicking a strap.

'It's called a teddy.'

He raised an eyebrow. 'My teddy never looked like that.'

Her soft laughter faded in the scorching heat of his embrace. Her heart was pounding but she had to touch him, to know the feel of his weight on her, to hold him close and welcome him to her body.

She lifted up her hands and cradled his face, pulling it down until she could reach his lips.

'Kiss me,' she whispered.

Then his fragile control shattered and he plundered her mouth with his, searching for her response and finding it in full measure while his hands explored her body and made her ache with frustration.

'I want you,' he whispered harshly, dragging his mouth away from hers and holding her hard against his heaving chest. 'God help me, Jo, I want you. . .'

She eased away from him and walked to the bed,

then, easing off the straps of her teddy, she let it slither to the floor at her feet.

Turning back the quilt, she climbed on to the narrow bed and patted the sheet beside her.

He watched her for a long time, his face in shadow with the light behind him, then his hands went to his belt and he unfastened his trousers and peeled them off in one motion.

Where and when his shoes went she had no idea, but he was standing there in front of her, naked and aroused, and her mouth suddenly felt dry.

He was thin, but he was still magnificent, a dark scatter of hair in the centre of his chest arrowing down over the hard, flat planes of his abdomen, his legs long and lean, well muscled but not heavy, carrying him towards her.

The bed dipped under his weight and then she was touching him, chest to chest, hip to hip, toe to toe, their bodies tangled as they touched and sighed and kissed in a wild dance that left them both shaken with emotion.

Gradually their breathing slowed and their bodies became their own again. They slept for a while, then Jo woke and found the bed empty.

'Alex?' she called.

'In here,' he said, his voice subdued.

She slipped out of bed and padded through to the sitting-room.

He was sitting on the sofa, his wallet in his hands, and as she came in he snapped it shut and stuffed it back into his jacket.

His cheeks were wet, and her eyes filled with tears for his pain.

'Alex?' she whispered.

He looked up at her, and then with a groan he was on his feet and she was in his arms, crushed against his chest as if he was afraid to let her go.

'Come on,' she said gently, and led him back to bed. There she held him and ran her hands down his back, trying to soothe away whatever pain it was that haunted him.

His lips found hers in the half-dark, and this time it was different, less desperate, more a sort of wooing.

It sounded crazy, but she almost felt that he was paying homage to her with his gentle touch and the subtle power of his kiss. It was almost like a thanksgiving. Whatever, his tenderness was overwhelming, and she came apart under his clever, gentle hands, only dimly aware of the violence of his own release.

They fell asleep curled together like spoons, and in Jo's heart was a deep peace and contentment such as she had never known.

She slept deeply until late in the morning, waking to a feeling of well-being that for the first few seconds she was unable to place.

Then she remembered, and reached for him in the narrow bed, only to sit up with a cold, sick feeling of dread washing over her.

The flat felt quiet—too quiet.

She ran through into the living-room, then checked the bathroom and the kitchen. She even looked in the hall cupboard before she would admit it to herself.

He was gone.

There was a note, of course, tucked under a faded rose probably pinched from her neighbour's garden.

It said, quite simply, 'Thank you. Alex.'

She screwed it up in a ball and flushed it down the loo before giving in to the temptation to burst into tears.

It was her own fault—she should have known better than to let herself be lured by a stranger with desolation in his eyes.

Perhaps in some small way she had given him a respite from the misery that he carried with him. Maybe. Hopefully. She hoped to God he had gained something positive, because during the night she had given him her heart.

She thought sadly that there was nothing more she could give him.

She was wrong.

The following week she started at the Audley Memorial, and in Owen Davie found a friend as well as a mentor.

He and his wife welcomed her to the hospital, and she settled in quickly, putting her encounter with Alex behind her.

She didn't notice in the hustle and bustle of the move and finding her feet in the new job that she had missed a period, but after a few weeks it dawned on her that she was probably pregnant.

A part of her was appalled, but the other and major part was ecstatic at the thought of Alex's child growing within her.

Then ten weeks after their encounter, tragedy struck.

She was in Theatre assisting Owen when a wave of nausea overcame her. She had been plagued by discomfort and morning sickness for a few weeks, and so she ignored the signals from her body and continued with the operation.

As they were closing up Owen turned to her and his brow creased in a frown.

'Are you OK, Jo?' he asked quietly. 'You look a bit green.'

'I feel it,' she admitted weakly. 'Actually, there's something I have to tell you.'

He gave her a slight smile. 'I think I can guess. We'll talk later.'

'I think that would be a good idea,' she said, but her attempted smile was wrenched from her lips as a sudden shaft of pain rocked through her.

She collapsed against Owen as another wave of nausea washed over her, and then within seconds blissful unconsciousness claimed her.

When she awoke she was tucked up in a hosptial bed, and a worried nurse rushed to fetch Owen to her bedside.

He was very sweet to her, but there was no way to soften what he had to tell her. She had suffered an ectopic pregnancy, and, because of the position of the foetus when her tube had ruptured, her uterus had been badly torn.

The damage had been all the more severe because her uterus had been malformed, probably causing the ectopic pregnancy in the first place, and would not have sustained a pregnancy. In order to save her life he had removed it to arrest the haemorrhage.

So that was that. Her dream was over. No baby, and no second chance.

After a few days in hospital she was sent home to convalesce, and only the memory of Alex's tender loving kept her from going insane.

He had wanted her, needed her. She was lovable—

she was. Alex had loved her, although he had left her so abruptly, but he must have had his reasons.

Bit by bit her sanity returned and with it her drive and determination.

The gutsy courage that would have made her a wonderful single parent emerged instead to sustain her and to direct her in the forging of her career.

She delved deeper into technique, getting involved in controversial new methods of labour management and even introducing a birthing-room and aromatherapy to the delivery suites.

She met her boss head-on over many of these issues. Some she won, some she lost, but throughout she fought with a single-mindedness that earned her a reputation not many women would have envied.

Slowly, brick by brick, she rebuilt her life, and when Owen announced that he was leaving to take on the post of professor of obstetrics in a London teaching hospital, she had applied for his job, confident that she would get it.

And then Alex had appeared, taking not only the job but also her peace of mind.

And all she wanted to do was crawl into his arms and weep the bitter tears that had been dammed up for too long.

She remembered a woman once who had lost a child, and, when Jo said to the social worker that the woman would feel better if she could only cry, the social worker had shaken her head sadly.

'Some things are too deep to cry about,' she told Jo.

How true. Tears solved nothing, changed nothing, but how she ached to lay the weight of her grief down at Alex's feet and ask him to heal her.

CHAPTER FOUR

Jo WAS on call that weekend, and on Saturday morning she was summoned to attend a girl of fifteen who was in early labour.

She arrived at the hospital just as Alex drew up in his dark blue Rover, and she shot him an enquiring glance.

He raised an eyebrow.

'Coming in to do some paperwork—is that OK?' he asked mildly.

'Of course it's OK,' she snapped. Poor man, he didn't deserve her temper, but she'd had a rotten night rehashing the past and he had figured too largely as the villain of the piece for her to greet him pleasantly.

'Got a problem?' he asked now as they walked together towards the lift.

'I don't know. We've got a young girl in labour—I haven't seen her before so I won't know until I do.'

He nodded. 'I'm around if you need me.'

'Why should I need you?' she asked crossly.

He sighed with exasperation. 'No reason, I was just trying to be helpful. Forget it.'

The lift arrived, and they travelled up in a tense silence. He got out at the third floor, and she heaved a sigh of relief as the lift carried her on up to the ward.

Anne Gabriel met her at the nurses' station. 'Hi. She's in there—I've called Maggie Wells up as she's a minor. I'm just waiting for her to come.'

'OK. Can you fill me in?'

It seemed that the girl, Karen Maxwell, was still only fifteen and her mother was ranting about loose morals and bad lots and generally carrying on, while Karen lay tearfully on the bed in sullen silence.

'Right,' Jo said briskly. 'The first thing we've got to do is get the mother out of there and tell her that if she can't give her daughter support then she'd better stay out until it's all over. The next thing is, how's her labour progressing? Do we need to alert Theatre? How big is she?'

'Almost at term, but she's a tiny little girl, Jo. I'm not sure she'll make it through labour without help.'

Jo ran her eye over Anne, whose slight frame had carried Beth and whose own delivery had been a nightmare of mismanagement and fear culminating in a nasty forceps delivery. She could understand how Anne felt about allowing Karen to go through the same experience, but she didn't want to rush her into a section.

'I'll have a look. First I'm getting the dragon out.'

She opened the door and walked briskly in. 'Good morning, Mrs Maxwell. I'm Joanna Harding, and I'll be looking after your daughter. I wonder if I could ask you to wait outside while I examine her and have a chat?'

'I'm not leaving,' the woman vowed. 'She'll tell you all her lies if I'm not here to keep her on the straight and narrow—lying little slut. Take your eyes off her for a minute and she'll steal the clothes off your back—and as for that nigger she took up with——!'

She gave an eloquent sniff, and glared at her daugher.

'I always said he'd get you in trouble, and now look at you! Dirty little whore. Got your just desserts at last——'

'Mrs Maxwell, I'm going to have to ask you to leave for a few minutes,' Jo said firmly, and, gripping the woman's arm, she steered her towards the door. A nurse was passing, and Jo called her, passed Mrs Maxwell to her—almost literally—and shot back inside.

'Anne, lean on the door and don't let her back in,' she ordered in an undertone, and went over to the bed.

'Hi, Karen. How're you doing?' she asked gently.

Karen rolled her eyes. 'Miserable old bag,' she mumbled tearfully. 'Hates my guts, she does. I'd leave if I had anywhere to go.'

Jo patted her hand. 'Let's just get through today, eh? Could I have a look and see how you're doing?'

She positioned the girl on her back and made a gentle but thorough examination to establish her progress. She checked the notes to see when her labour had started, and listened to the baby's heart during a contraction.

'Well, everything seems to be fine so far, but just to be on the safe side I want to link you up to a monitor for a little while that will tell me how the baby's doing as the time passes, OK? It won't hurt—it's just a band that goes round your tummy, but it isn't very comfortable, so it's important for you to relax as much as possible. Has anybody shown you any breathing exercises?'

Karen shook her head slowly. 'Nobody's shown me anything. I know what's going on a bit, because of biology lessons at school, and I know how I ended up here, but that's about the limit. Mum won't talk about it and Damien doesn't know anything more than I do.'

'Damien?'

'My fella—look, Doctor, can I see him?'

Jo exchanged glances with Anne. The whole scenario was so irregular that Anne was out of her depth.

'I should think so, for a minute or two. How can we get hold of him?'

'I think he might be here,' Anne said quietly. 'Is he tall, Afro-Caribbean, about eighteen?'

Karen nodded. 'Yeah—he's got a scar on his chin.'

'That's him. He's in the waiting-room. I'll get him.'

She opened the door and immediately they could hear raised voices from the other end of the corridor.

'Oh, cripes, Mum's seen him,' Karen muttered.

'I'll go,' Jo said grimly. 'What's his surname?'

'Jackson.'

'Right.' She swept up the corridor, her white coat billowing out behind her, and entered the waiting-room with a flourish. Karen's mother and a tall black boy were standing facing each other, yelling, while a young nurse fruitlessly attempted to mediate.

At her entry they all swung in her direction.

'Please keep your voices down; there are babies trying to sleep on the ward,' she told them firmly. 'Mrs Maxwell, Karen seems to be all right at the moment, but it will be some time before she makes very much progress. Perhaps it would be as well if you went and had a cup of coffee in the canteen—the sister can give you a ticket.'

She waited while the harassed nurse escorted the woman out, muttering under her breath, and then she swivelled her attention to Damien, who was standing glaring out of the window, his hands rammed into the pockets of his jeans.

'Mr Jackson? Karen would like to see you for a minute, if you'd care to come with me?'

She gave the disbelieving youth an encouraging smile, and led him down the ward to the little side room where Karen was lying on the bed. She looked very young and very frightened, and her face brightened visibly when he went in.

'Are you OK, love?' he asked gently, and, taking her hands, he sat beside her and rubbed her fingers absently while he watched her.

At that moment a contraction gripped her, and she tensed her body and cried out with the pain. An expression of anguish crossed his face, and he glanced helplessly at Jo.

'What can I do?' he asked her.

Jo stifled the impulse to tell him that he could usefully have thought of that nine months ago, and told him instead to encourage her to relax. 'I'll get a midwife to come and explain the principles of relaxation to you both, and then you can help her with her breathing, if you want to stay.'

He nodded urgently. 'Please don't make me leave her,' he begged.

'We'll see how it goes,' Jo told him, and then took Anne out into the corridor.

'He seems a nice enough lad,' Anne said.

Jo snorted. 'Irresponsible young fool, more like. Where's Maggie?'

'Here's Maggie. What's the prob?'

They turned round and smiled at the newcomer. Her long red-gold hair was looped up in a pony-tail, and, with her early morning face bare of make-up, she didn't look a great deal older than Karen. She had deep shadows under her eyes that matched the blue irises almost exactly, a fact that Jo commented on with candid good humour.

'Yes, well, it's been a rotten week. So what's going on down here?'

'We've got a minor in Labour. Mother's been an obnoxious pain in the neck, the youth responsible is in with the girl belatedly wondering how he can help her, and we need paediatric cover for the labour.'

'Just another routine Saturday morning,' Maggie said with a laugh, and opened the door.

'Hello, there, I'm Dr Wells—I'm the paediatrician on call today. Everything OK?'

Jo left them to it, and went and spoke to the midwife who was covering Karen and another woman whose labour was much further advanced.

When she had time she nipped up and gave Karen and Damien instructions on breathing and relaxation, and also some lavender oil to massage on to her back and tummy to ease the contractions.

Jo, at a loose end for a while and obviously not urgently required, left Anne Gabriel in charge and wandered out to the stairwell. The lift was moving, and she saw the light on three. Alex's floor. She chewed her lip. Had it been Owen, she would have thought nothing of going and discussing Karen's case with him, but somehow Alex was different. Their whole relationship was different, and casual chats were almost impossible to conduct under the strain of their mutual feelings.

With a heavy sigh she turned back and saw Maggie coming towards her.

'She's doing OK, isn't she? You don't really need me—although she's a child, she quite evidently isn't, really. A sort of tragic half-child. I gather the mother's the pits.'

Jo's mouth lifted in a rueful smile. 'Just a touch.'

'You know, she could be taken into care and then she wouldn't have to live with her. If Mum gets difficult during the delivery, give me a ring and we can have Karen taken into care instantly if necessary.'

Jo nodded. 'Thanks, Maggie. I'll call if I need you.'

She watched as the young woman ran lightly down the stairs, despite her evident tiredness. With a slight smile, Jo turned back to the ward.

Karen's progress was slow but sure. Damien was terrific, supporting her through all her contractions, refusing to leave her side, ignoring the mother's constant criticism.

Jo sent Anne home to Beth, and during the course of the afternoon she attended two other deliveries and kept an eye on Karen's progress.

Late that afternoon she began to worry. Although the baby's head was well down and Karen's cervix was dilating steadily, she was getting tired, and Jo wasn't sure if she could make it on her own.

She wished she could talk to Owen. It wasn't that she lacked the necessary experience or ability, but decisions were often easier to make in the light of discussion.

Maggie popped up again to see how things were progressing, and Jo confided her uncertainty in her.

'So ask the head honcho,' she said with a shrug.

'Ask the head honcho what?' came a deep voice from behind them, and Jo sighed. What was he still doing in the hospital?

Maggie flushed and grinned at him. 'Hi, Mr Carter.'

He winced. 'That's very ageing,' he complained gently.

'Serve you right—it goes with the territory,' Jo told him laughingly. 'And what makes you think we were talking about you?'

He raised an eyebrow laconically. 'Got a problem?'

Jo shrugged. 'Sort of—bye, Maggie. See you later.' They watched her walk away, and then Alex turned back to Jo.

'Sort of?'

'The minor—Karen Maxwell. She's making fairly heavy weather of it. I don't think she's got a primary hypotonia, because her contractions were fairly strong earlier, but she's getting very tired. There's no sign of foetal distress, but I just don't know if we should let her go on, and how long for. She's very young, and I think she's been punished enough for her mistake without us making her delivery a misery unnecessarily. And the mother's being a total pain in the butt, furthermore.'

As they walked down the ward, Jo filled him in on the details, and, as they approached the room, Jo could hear the raised voices.

'Oh, not again!' she muttered.

'We'll soon stop that,' Alex said firmly, and pushed open the door.

'Mrs Maxwell, is it, and Mr Jackson? My name's Carter, and I'm the consultant in charge of Miss

Maxwell. I wonder if I might ask you both to step outside for a few minutes?'

'I'm not going anywhere with him!' Mrs Maxwell protested with a glare at Damien, but Alex would brook no argument and ushered the pair of them out.

'Right, Karen, let's see how things are going, eh?'

He examined her deftly, studied the charts, and nodded to Jo. 'Steady, but slow, isn't it? Are you getting tired, Karen?'

The girl nodded wearily. 'It wouldn't be so bad if Mum would shut up, but she's ranting on all the time——'

'We'll keep her out, don't worry. What about your young man?'

'Can he stay?'

'If that's what you want,' Alex agreed. 'The important thing is that you're relaxed. How would you feel about having an epidural—that's an injection into your back to numb the lower half of your body, so you don't feel the pain, and we could then give you a drug to speed things up a bit?'

She gave a helpless little shrug. 'I dunno—I just wish it was all over. . .'

Huge, heavy tears started to roll down her cheeks, and the midwife hitched herself up on to the bed and hugged her to her motherly bosom.

'There, there, love. Don't take on so. Come on, there's a good girl.'

Alex shook his head. 'Poor bloody kid,' he muttered under his breath. 'Right, we'll get the mother to sign the consent form and we can get the epidural under way if necessary. She may need forceps, as well. Better cover it all on the form.'

But Mrs Maxwell was adamant. 'Why should I sign it? Serve the little slag right if she suffers. Dirty little tart—and as for you, you wicked, cradle-snatching filthy nigger——'

Alex's face contracted in cold fury. 'Mrs Maxwell, we are talking about your daughter. Now for heaven's sake pull yourself together and calm down! If you don't sign the consent form, we will be unable to give her the help she needs.'

'So?'

'So we can have her taken into care, and, if you ask me, she'd be better off!' he retorted angrily.

'You can't do that; it's against the law!'

He looked grimly at her. 'Will you sign?'

'No.'

'So be it. Damien, Karen would like you with her. Mrs Maxwell, I would be grateful if you would stay here—the social worker will be along to talk to you as soon as possible.'

'What social worker? Hey, I don't want no social worker poking her nose in——'

Alex turned on his heel and followed Damien out, Jo close behind.

He marched down the ward to the sister's office, snatched up the phone and asked for the medical social worker to be paged.

She appeared within minutes, contacted the magistrate, and within half an hour Karen was in the care of the social services department, the consent form was signed and the anaesthetist was on standby.

Mrs Maxwell was raging in the waiting-room, and in the end the police came and took her away.

In the meantime Jo and Alex themselves were arguing about the management of Karen's labour. She was obviously making less and less progress, and Alex wanted to hasten the proceedings with an epidural, a drip and forceps if necessary. Jo, on the other hand, wanted to get Karen up and walk her round, put her in a hot bath, get Damien rubbing her back and tummy with lavender oil and generally stimulate her uterus back into action.

'It's her first experience, Alex, and given the right help it could be a marvellous one——'

'Marvellous? Dragging on for hour after hour until she's too exhausted to care one way or the other? Come on, Jo!'

'I'm serious!' she argued. 'All that unnecessary intervention could put her off for life——'

'Let's face it,' Alex put in drily, 'it wouldn't be a bad thing if it put her off for a while!'

Jo sighed with exasperation and ran her hands through her wildly tangled hair. 'Putting people off childbirth doesn't stop them getting pregnant!' she told him crossly, then her temper drained and she sat down with a bump. 'All I'm asking for is a chance for her, Alex. Just give me more time, please?'

He studied her in silence for a while, and then nodded. 'OK. We'll use the portable monitor, and as long as there's no danger to the baby and Karen's able to tolerate it, we'll do it your way. But I'm warning you——'

'Bless you!' Jo leapt to her feet and hugged him impulsively, then strode back across the corridor into Karen's room.

Karen was oblivious. Damien had stayed with her while the social worker had done her stuff, and his quiet presence seemed to be her anchor in the unreality of a world gone mad.

Alex followed her, and they studied Karen's progress on a partogram, a graph that compared her progress with the average progress of normal women of her population group. Her labour was shown quite clearly to be slower than was expected by some considerable margin.

The midwife, Sue, was familiar with Jo's techniques, and was more than willing to help chivvy things along.

While she ran a deep, warm bath and encouraged Karen to walk around, Jo and Alex took a much needed break and went along to the ward kitchen to make a cup of tea and a pile of hot buttered toast. They sat at the table sharing a plate and talking over the case, and then Alex switched the subject unexpectedly.

'It was the infertility clinic yesterday,' he said. 'It was hectic. I could do with another pair of hands to help.'

Jo shrugged. 'Funding's difficult. We're lucky to be able to offer it at all. Of course there's no chance we'll be able to do IVF for a good while, unless a miracle happens, but the patients at least get the preliminaries out of the way. But there's no chance of taking on any help, I don't think.'

Alex stirred his tea thoughtfully. 'I was hoping you'd give me a hand—perhaps an hour, once a week? Even that would make a difference. They want to talk, and there just isn't time. It makes it all so clinical, so unfeeling. In Surrey we had counsellors and much more back-up, but here they get ushered in, asked a few questions, given another piece of barbaric equipment to go and play with and an appointment to come back in a couple of months—really, it's hopeless. And to make a difference, I need your help.'

Jo swallowed, her heart pounding. 'I'd rather not, if you don't mind. I have a lot on my plate as it is——'

'Don't we all? Come on, Jo, please. I really need your backing on this.'

'I—infertility clinics aren't really my thing, Alex.'

He snorted. 'If you'd got the job, you wouldn't have had a choice.'

'But I didn't, did I? So I have the choice.'

'Oh, for God's sake, what is it with you? Surely to God you aren't a prude?'

She laughed uncomfortably, but she couldn't look at him. 'Don't be absurd, of course I'm not——'

'Then what?'

He was waiting, but she couldn't tell him. 'Do I have to have a reason?' she asked.

'Damn right you do! Jo, those people need help— do you have any idea what they're going through? What it must be like to want a child so badly that you can't sleep at night or concentrate on your work for thinking about it? What kind of heartless bitch are you that you can't give a little of your time to help them? Haven't you got any imagination?'

The heavy ache in her heart seemed to swell until she could hardly breathe. Any imagination? Damn it, she didn't *need* imagination to know what they were going through! Pushing back her chair, she stood up abruptly.

'I'm going to see how Karen's getting on,' she mumbled, and left him sitting in confusion.

A few minutes later he joined her, and their row was

forgotten as they assessed Karen's progress. Her contractions were stronger, and the midwife was confident that things were now moving.

'Excellent,' Jo said with a smile. 'Keep walking, Karen, and Damien, keep hold of her. She may need to lean on you.'

He nodded, his face serious. 'That's why I'm here,' he said, and, with his arm around Karen, he walked her slowly round the room.

Alex disappeared to his study with instructions for them to contact him if necessary.

After that things hotted up, and soon Karen was moved to the delivery-room and shown how to use the Entonox machine.

With Damien's support and the midwife and Jo working together to encourage and instruct her, Karen managed to deliver her baby without any help except for a small episiotomy.

As the head crowned, Jo was aware of Alex at her side, and as the baby made his appearance into the world Jo lifted him in capable hands and laid him over Karen's tummy.

'You've got a son, Karen,' Jo told her, her voice husky, and she somehow managed to return Damien's dazzling smile.

'Thank God,' he said unsteadily, and then huge tears cascaded down his cheeks. He dashed them away with the backs of his hands and touched his son with aching tenderness. 'Well done,' he murmured to Karen, and, bending down, he kissed her gently on the lips. Then, heedless of the mess, he kissed his son's brow.

Jo dragged her eyes away from their private moment and stared out of the window into the darkness. In the distance, far below, she could see lights twinkling across the town, and behind her Karen and Damien's baby son was yelling his protest.

'Beautiful, isn't it?' Alex said in her ear.

They both knew he wasn't talking about the night.

Jo nodded, unable to speak.

'Just imagine what it must be like to know that you can never experience that joy,' he added softly. 'To know that, no matter what, that gift will never be yours. How can you turn away from them, Jo?'

She closed her eyes. 'All right, Alex, you win,' she sighed. 'I'll help you with your damn infertility clinic.'

At least, she thought, she would be able to understand their grief.

Straightening her shoulders, she turned back to her patient.

At one o'clock on Monday morning she was called out again, but for a very different sort of delivery.

This was a local GP and his wife, a young, healthy woman of twenty-five who was having her first baby. Her labour was proceeding nicely, and the only reason Jo was there at all was that it was hospital policy to have a senior member of staff available to deliver 'medical' babies—one of the perks of the profession, so to speak—and Alex was not on duty.

She found them in a side-ward, both sitting on the edge of the bed, arms round each other.

'Hello, there. How's it going? I'm Jo Harding.'

The man stood up, not much taller than Jo, solidly built with an open, handsome face and tortoiseshell glasses masking a pair of spectacularly blue eyes.

'Sorry to get you out of bed,' he said with a grin, and

extended his hand. 'Matt Gregory, and this is my wife Polly.'

Jo leant over and shook his hand, then hers. 'Hi. Hello, Mrs Gregory. How are you coping?'

She smiled, a lovely serene smile that lit her warm brown eyes and dimpled her soft cheeks. 'Oh, fine— Matt's been rubbing my back with lavender oil, and he's helping me with the breathing and keeping me sane generally.'

She chuckled softly, and he laughed and squeezed her hand.

'She's doing really well. I'm very proud of her.'

Jo scanned the charts and nodded. 'OK, that looks fine. When were you last examined?'

'I haven't been, yet. Well, Matt looked at me before we left home, but I've only been here a few minutes.'

'Right, I'll get a midwife and a trolley and we'll take a look at you.'

She went out into the corridor and was surprised to see Alex walking towards her. He looked exhausted.

'Hi,' she said, 'what brings you in?'

'I've just finished off some paperwork—I didn't realise it was so late.'

She glanced at her watch. It was half-past one. 'If you don't go home to bed you'll be useless next week.'

He laughed humourlessly. 'Quite likely. I can't sleep anyway. Every time I close my eyes I see you.'

'Alex, don't,' she begged.

'I don't want to,' he told her bluntly. 'You're a good doctor, but you lack warmth, Jo. God knows what I see in you, but every time I shut my eyes I can picture you standing in that sordid little flat stripping off your clothes for me, and I want you.'

Jo closed her eyes against the image. 'Alex, stop it,' she breathed.

'Why? Because you want me too?' A nurse bustled past and gave them a curious glance, and he seemed to collect himself. 'What are you doing here?'

'Local GP's wife.'

'VIP treatment? Want me to lend it a little weight?' he asked with self-derision.

She sighed. She hated him in this mood. 'If you wish,' she told him.

'Not really,' he confessed, 'but I'm around if you need me.'

After examining Polly, Jo asked her if they had any particular feelings about the conduct of her labour and delivery.

Polly nodded. 'You've got a birthing-room, is that right?'

'Yes, we have a room with a birthing-chair, stereo system, bath, mattresses on the floor, thigh rings—all sorts of things. You can do whatever you like.'

'I wanted to have the baby at home, but Matt threw a monumental fit. I suppose he's right, because I'm only small, but I just want to be able to do what I want to do—I don't know yet what I will want, but will I have the freedom to do it?'

'Of course,' Jo assured her. 'The birthing-room's free now, so if you want to move in there you're more than welcome. You can lie, sit, stand, walk around, have a bath, sing, cry—whatever you want. The only thing we ask is enough light to deliver the baby safely. Once we're sure everything's fine, we turn it down again. And if things get tricky, the delivery-room with all the necessary equipment is next door, and the theatre is always on standby. OK?'

They nodded, and the midwife, Beverley, took them into the birthing-room and settled them down.

Jo went to get a cup of tea and saw Alex in the nursery, a baby cradled in his arms, feeding it from a bottle. He had taken off his jacket and his sleeves were rolled up, and as she watched his mouth curved in a tender smile.

She realised with a jolt that it was the first time she had seen him really smile, and the knowledge stabbed her like a knife. That it was a baby of all things that had brought the smile to his lips was another bitter twist of fate.

Forgetting her tea, she went back to see how Polly was doing. It was quiet in the birthing-room, soft music playing gently in the background, and the aroma of lavender oil scenting the air. The lighting was dim, and the whole atmosphere was very restful.

They were on the floor on a mattress. Polly, dressed in a soft old cotton shirt several sizes too big for her, was kneeling on all fours and swaying gently to the music, and Matt knelt behind her, his hands making slow, lazy circles on her bare back. She paused to pant, and his hands slid round under her and soothed the ripe curve of her belly as she sagged back against him.

Then she moved again, sighing deeply, and his hands came back round and over her hips, starting the slow circles again.

He looked up and smiled.

'How's it going?' Jo asked.

'One and a half minutes on, one and a half minutes

off. I don't think she'll be long,' he told her, his voice
a deep, melodic rumble in the quiet room.

'I feel sick,' Polly said suddenly, and he grabbed a
bowl and held her head and soothed her with wordless
little noises until she had finished.

Things moved quickly after that. Jo sent a nurse for
Alex, and he came in and stood quietly, still in his
shirt-sleeves, as Polly sat on the birthing chair and
started to push.

After a few minutes she looked up at her husband in
desperation and reached out to him.

'I want to stand—I have to!' she cried, and he lifted
her to the mattress on the floor and hooked her arms
around his neck and held her as she hung on him and
strained.

It was an absolutely natural, spontaneous and very
touching delivery, despite the crowd. The midwife was
there, and Jo and Alex, and as the baby was born Matt
lowered Polly to the mattress and took his daughter
from the midwife, lifting her to Polly's breast.

Their eyes were both bright with tears, and Jo had
to look away. So much joy was a little hard to handle.

By the time she had cleared up and the placenta was
delivered and checked and the baby washed and
dressed and back in Polly's arms, she had had about all
she could take.

Slipping out of the birthing-room, she washed in the
sluice and went up to the ward kitchen to make herself
a cup of tea.

Alex was in there, but it was too late to change her
mind and go past the door, and anyway she was
desperate for a cup of tea.

He passed her one without a word, and she took it equally silently and sank down gratefully at the table.

'Very touching,' he said drily.

'Don't denigrate it,' Jo defended. 'Lots of people have used that room in the same way and been very grateful for its presence.'

'I'm not denigrating it,' he told her quietly, 'but it's unrealistic. For the vast majority of people that sort of delivery is unattainable. I just wonder if we couldn't make a better use of the resources tied up in it.'

She sighed and rolled her eyes. 'I've had this fight before——'

'And won it—for now. Are you OK?'

She glared at him. 'Of course I'm OK—why shouldn't I be?'

He shrugged. 'Pass. You just looked——'

'Not again,' she muttered, and pushed away her tea. She left Alex clearing up and went into the duty officer's room and shut the door, then stared unblinkingly at her reflection in the tatty little mirror. In the unrelenting glare of the overhead light she looked ravaged and tear-streaked. She hadn't realised she, too, had cried.

Perhaps she was torturing herself unnecessarily. If she changed to another specialisation, she wouldn't have to go through this, but obstetrics was her greatest love and she couldn't imagine doing anything else now.

There was a bed in the room and she turned off the overhead light and lay down, leaving on the bedside light in case she woke. If anyone needed her, they could bleep her, but she couldn't stand another confrontation with Alex tonight.

She was in the strange no man's land halfway

between sleep and wakefulness when he came in and sat on the edge of the bed.

She forced herself to wake up. 'How's Polly?' she asked him. Her voice sounded husky and sultry.

'She's fine. They all are. Are you OK?'

'Of course—just a bit tired. I couldn't be bothered going home this late. Why are you still here?'

'Finishing off this and that—I just wondered where you were.' He brushed her cheek with his knuckles. 'You looked—how you always look when anyone has a baby.' He hesitated, and then went on quietly, 'I think I've misjudged you. I thought you were heartless, but you're not, you're a pussycat. The only other answer is that you really want children, and you can't have them.'

Her heart thudding, Jo looked away from him. Surely he couldn't have found out?

'What makes you say that?' she asked, her voice strained.

'Look at you, Jo,' he murmured. 'You're all woman. You're a real earth mother, and you love babies. I've watched you talking to Anne Gabriel about Beth, and you really care about her. You'd be a wonderful mother, if only you weren't so stubborn.' His hand opened and his fingers rested softly against her throat. 'Plenty of women marry and have babies and carry on their careers, Jo. You wouldn't have to give it up.'

'Not me,' she said, relief flooding her that his remarks had been based on wildly incorrect assumptions. 'I can't get married and have children and keep on my job—I'm not that sort of woman,' she said truthfully.

'What sort of woman are you, Jo?' he asked softly.

'One minute I think I know you, and the next I realise I don't know you at all. All I can be sure of is that I want to know you better.'

She looked up at him and their eyes meshed as his head came down and blocked out the light. Her eyes fluttered closed as his lips brushed against hers. Her arms climbed up all by themselves and wrapped around his neck, and with a groan of resignation she gave herself up to his kiss.

After an age he lifted his head and smoothed the hair back from her brow.

'I've got to get out of here,' he murmured huskily. 'This bed is too damn tempting. What are you doing tomorrow evening?'

Too late, she collected her wits. 'Alex, I thought you'd agreed——'

'I agreed nothing,' he argued softly. 'But just to set your mind at rest, I'm house-hunting. I wanted your opinion on a couple I've short-listed. I'd hate to buy a house with the wrong address,' he joked lightly. 'Are you free?'

'Yes, I——'

'Good. We can have dinner afterwards. I'll pick you up at seven.'

And with a quick kiss on her brow, he was gone, leaving her floundering in indecision, partly about whether or not she had any marbles left at all, but mainly about what on earth she would wear!

CHAPTER FIVE

AFTER checking that all was well on the ward at seven-thirty that morning, Jo went home to shower and change ready for the day. After years of practice, lack of sleep didn't really bother her much any more, at least not after one night, but she was finding her job more emotionally draining since Alex's appearance on the scene than she had ever done before.

Her personal situation hadn't really made that much difference to her until now, because there hadn't been anybody who made her want to have the things that were out of reach, but in the last week every birth had registered ten on the Richter scale and she was feeling somewhat shaken up.

He wasn't around much that morning, as he had a list, so she was able to check on Polly Gregory and Karen Maxwell without his input.

Polly was blooming, delighted with her little daughter Alice and full of the joys of spring. She had enjoyed her delivery and was set for a very quick recovery. Her husband was picking them up that evening and taking them home, and Polly was obviously going to be able to cope easily with an early discharge. A nurse herself, and married to a GP, she would hardly lack advice, she said drily to Jo.

Jo was glad things had gone so well. She had a feeling that Polly was an incurable optimist, and if things had gone wrong her illusions would have been badly shattered.

Karen, on the other hand, was recovering only slowly from her tiring labour and delivery, and was content to stay in hospital as long as they would let her. She was to go into a home for young girls and their babies that had been set up by social services in response to the tragically obvious need for it, and would be able to keep her baby with her and look after him while continuing with her education under the care of a team of visiting teachers.

Damien, who was on probation as a result of his relationship with Karen, was working a late shift and so was in with Karen that morning. He was sitting in the chair with his son in his arms, his finger held in a vice-like grip by the little lad, exploring the delights of eye contact.

Karen had slipped out to the bathroom, so Jo perched herself on the end of the bed and asked him what plans if any he had for the future.

'We intend to get married as soon as she's sixteen,' he said, and then shrugged at Jo's compassionate and reproachful look.

'You can't call me anything or think anything that the police and the magistrate and the social workers and my probation officer haven't already said, and, anyway, none of it touches what I've called myself.' His voice was harsh with bitterness and self-condemnation, and Jo's heart reached out to him.

'How did it happen, Damien?'

He gave an embarrassed laugh. 'The usual way.'

Jo smiled. 'I meant her being so young.'

He sighed. 'She told me she was sixteen. I believed

her. You're not seeing her at her best—take my word
for it, she doesn't look fifteen when she's out at night!'

'I'm sure. What do you do?'

'I work in a factory, packing boxes. The money isn't
fantastic, but it's a job. Lots of my friends aren't as
well off.'

Jo stood up and ran her finger over the sleepy baby's
cheek. 'Well, I wish you all luck,' she said quietly. 'I
think you're going to need it.' With a sad smile she
walked away to tackle the ever present paperwork.

The rest of the day slipped quietly by in a constant
stream of examinations and consultations and deliveries and reassurances. By six she was ready to lie down
and sleep for a week, but instead she went home,
soaked in the bath for fifteen minutes and then dried
her hair and dressed quickly.

At five to seven the phone rang.

'I just realised I don't know where you live,' Alex
told her.

She gave him directions and then went downstairs to
tidy up the sitting-room. It was raining, she noticed
dispassionately. A few moments later his dark blue
Rover slid to a halt outside her cottage and he jumped
out and ran to the door.

She opened it immediately, shrugging her mac on as
she did so, and he helped her into it.

'All ready?' he asked, and she nodded. Flicking on
the outside light, she picked up her keys and shut the
door behind them.

His car was warm, and the leather seats were softly
supportive.

'Very posh,' she said, peering round.

He snorted. 'Hardly. I picked it up at auction. The mileage is horrendous, but it looks quite smart.'

'Got to protect your image, haven't you?' she teased, and to her surprise he flushed.

'Hey, I was joking!' she said. 'I like it.'

He shot her a dry look. 'The car or the image?'

She laughed, and to her utter amazement a slow smile lit his face. No matter that it was self-derisory, it was still a smile on those usually sombre features, and she felt as if she'd wrought a miracle.

Settling back into the seat, she returned his smile. 'So where are we going first?'

'I've narrowed it down to one,' he told her. 'I went out for a drive at lunchtime and went off the other one. This one's empty, so I could have it quickly if I want it.' A few minutes later he pulled up at the side of the road. 'Here we are—the key's in the glovebox.'

She opened the flap and found the key, then looked up at their surroundings.

They were parked in a broad, tree-lined avenue on the outskirts of town, with large Edwardian houses set back from the road and well spaced out. The house they were in front of looked as if it could do with a coat of paint, but it was wide and seemed enormous.

'Heavens, however big is it?'

'Three reception, kitchen, utility, five bedrooms, two bathrooms, half an acre of garden.'

'For you?'

He looked awkward for a moment, and then shrugged. 'I like space,' he said unconvincingly. 'Come on.'

Taking the key from her, he opened the door and held it for her. As she stepped into the hall and

breathed in the still, slightly musty air, she fell instantly
and irretrievably in love.

The pale oak-panelled hall was wide and spacious,
and to their left the stairs climbed in three short flights
past a stained-glass window to the galleried landing
above. To their right was a small room, probably a
study, and in front of them were two more rooms, the
bigger one on the right obviously the drawing-room,
the one beside it the dining-room. Both had french
doors out into the west-facing garden. The hall turned
left beyond the stairs and led past a cloakroom to the
kitchen which stretched the full depth of the house and
was in dire need of updating. The garage was beyond
the kitchen, with a utility-room of sorts behind it off
the kitchen, and upstairs there were three good-sized
bedrooms, two smaller ones and a bathroom, and a
small dressing-room off the master bedroom which
could easily be turned into another bathroom.

As they wandered from room to room, their footsteps unnaturally loud on the bare boards, Jo was
conscious of the essence of family life that still echoed
round the empty house.

In one of the little rooms there was a child's painting
still on the wall, yellowed with age and crumbling at
the edges, bearing the faded legend, 'Heidi, age 8'.

In the other one there was a name carved in the
doorframe, low down near the floor. Alex crouched
down and ran his finger over it. 'Thomas,' he
deciphered. 'Little rascal. I wonder if they were brother
and sister, or if he was an earlier contributor?'

Jo busied herself with the built-in cupboard in the
corner.

He straightened slowly. 'So, what do you think? Does it have potential?'

Jo turned away, disturbed by the light in his eyes. Surely he wasn't thinking—no, he had made his opinion of her more than clear. Although last night. . .

'Never mind about me—what do you think?'

'I love it.'

She nodded. 'It is a lovely house.'

She wasn't conscious of the wistful note in her voice, or the tired droop to her mouth, but she was certainly conscious of the need to escape.

'How about the garden?'

'We'll go and look, shall we?' Alex suggested easily, holding the door for her with the effortless good manners she was beginning to take for granted.

He unlocked the back door and they went out into the damp garden, fresh after the rain, and stood on the paved terrace looking over the broad sweep of what had once been lawn.

'Goodness, it needs some work,' Jo commented, her eye taking in the glorious mounds of perennials just going over now, and the bold splash of colour from the late-blooming roses clustered against the south-facing wall.

At the end of the garden was a small orchard heavy with fruit, with an old swing suspended from the boughs of a large apple tree, and behind the garage there was a small group of brick and timber outbuildings that they went to investigate. One was a privy complete with wooden seat, another a coal store, another still a tool store and workshop.

'Super for kids,' Alex said, and Jo couldn't decide if his remark was pointed or not. She rather hoped not.

Just then it started to rain again and he ushered her back inside, then, locking the doors, he ran to the car to open the door for her before crossing swiftly to his own side and sliding in behind the wheel.

'Phew! It's chucking it down!'

Jo watched him as he blotted his face and hair with a handkerchief.

'Of course, you wouldn't have got half so wet if you hadn't opened the door for me,' she said mischievously.

He laughed softly. 'Sorry, just habit. You're quite right, of course, and someone as self-opinionated as you probably deserves to be made to open her own door, but I'm just a dyed-in-the-wool chauvinist, I'm afraid.'

Jo smiled. 'Yes, I'm afraid you are.'

He returned her smile slowly, as if he was out of practice. 'Hungry?'

She nodded. 'Starving. Where are we going?'

He tapped the side of his nose. 'Secret.'

'Child,' she scolded, and he rewarded her with another smile.

Heavens, she thought, now he's remembered how he can't seem to stop!

He took her to a new restaurant in town, intimate and discreet, and after they had ordered they talked of this and that and nothing in particular, both consciously avoiding work and personal matters, until they had finished eating and their coffee had been set in front of them.

Then Alex said, 'So you think I should buy it, do you?'

'The house? If you like it. It isn't really up to me, is it?'

He stirred his coffee and didn't answer for a while.

'I'll get a surveyor's report,' he said finally. 'More coffee?'

'No, thank you. I could do with a fairly early night.'

'Me, too.' He lifted his hand and the waiter appeared instantly.

In the car, Jo told Alex about her conversation with Damien that morning. 'They've got so many difficulties piling up ahead of them, those two,' she said sadly.

'You can never guarantee that you won't have. Matt and Polly Gregory should be at home now with their daughter—I wonder how they'll get on?'

'They're obviously head over heels in love—they won't have any problems, Alex.'

He snorted. 'Being in love doesn't guarantee a damn thing, Jo, believe me.'

Something struck her. 'Are you divorced?' she asked him bluntly.

'No,' he replied, just as bluntly. 'I'm not divorced. Here we are.'

He pulled up outside her house and switched off the engine, but he made no move to get out.

'Thank you for coming to look at the house with me,' he said instead.

'My pleasure. I don't think you'll have any image problems with it—it's definitely the right address!'

He gave a humourless little laugh. 'It's a family house, isn't it—did you feel that?'

She couldn't answer. She didn't dare trust her voice.

'It got to you, didn't it? You looked at home there, Jo. It's your sort of house—not a pretty little bachelor cottage like this, but a big, bustling house with tumbling children and lots of visitors popping in and the smell of baking on the air——'

'Alex, for God's sake, leave me alone! You keep hammering on and on—it's not for me! And while we're on the subject, you go misty-eyed and gooey every time there's a delivery, and I saw you feeding that baby in the nursery last night—if you're so damn keen, why the hell aren't you at home with a cosy little wife and six kids instead of giving me all this strain?'

He looked away, but not before the dim glow of her outside light showed the old familiar anguish twist his features. Then he thrust open his door and climbed out, coming round to open her door and help her out.

'Alex?'

He was grimly silent, and she marched up to the front door and shoved the key into the lock. 'Don't answer, then,' she said shortly.

'Oh, I intend to answer you,' he told her heavily. 'There's a lot to tell you, and it's high time I did. It's just knowing where to start.'

She held the door open. 'You'd better come in. Take a seat—I'll put the kettle on.'

When she rejoined him she found him fossicking quietly among her music collection.

'Eclectic taste,' he said drily.

'Put whatever you like on,' she told him, and, shutting the curtains, she switched on the lamps and turned off the top light.

The soft strains of contemporary jazz poured out of the speakers in a soothing stream.

'Nice place you've got here.'

'Thank you. You're procrastinating.'

He met her eyes, and nodded slowly. 'Yes—yes, I am. As I said, it's knowing where to start.'

'The beginning?'

He sat on a chair, his feet braced apart, his elbows resting on his knees.

She sat on the floor, near him, not too close, but close enough. It was so quiet that she could hear the sound of his breathing over the soft music. Finally he started to speak, very quietly, and she had to strain to hear.

'When I was twenty-six and doing my house year, I met a girl called Cathy. She was sweet and pretty, and I fell in love. It was a hell of a year, but, when it was ended, I married her, and we moved to Reading. I did my registration year at the Royal Berks, and she worked as an agency nurse, and for the first few months everything was wonderful. We made plans—buying a cottage in the country, two point four kids, a couple of Labradors—you name it, we planned it. Then Cathy started getting very tired. I thought it was the work, so, although we couldn't really afford for her to stop, she gave up nursing.'

He sighed. 'Perhaps if I hadn't been so busy I would have noticed the other little signs, but I didn't. Then one day she was out shopping and she fainted. They brought her into the hospital and sent for me.' He paused. 'She had leukaemia. At first she had transfusions and chemotherapy and it held her in remission for months at a time, but then the intervals started getting shorter, and the relapses longer. We moved to London so she could get to the Royal Marsden more easily, and they tried bone-marrow transplants and God knows what else.'

He swallowed and looked hard at his hands. 'It took three years to kill her. Three long, lonely, bloody years.'

'Oh, Alex, I'm so sorry. . .'

He looked up and met her eyes. 'That's why I left you that night. It was the first anniversary of her death. I had nothing to offer you. I told you I went back three weeks later to make sure you weren't pregnant—it's a good job you weren't, because I would have married you out of some misguided sense of duty and I would have made you miserable, but that night I couldn't have walked away from you if my life depended on it. You were the light at the end of a long, dark tunnel that seemed to stretch back forever. I honestly think if I hadn't met you that night I wouldn't have made it to the morning.'

'Oh, my love. . .'

She moved towards him, but he held up his hand.

'Don't, Jo. Not unless you're going to follow through.'

She froze for a moment, unbearably tempted, but then sanity reared its ugly head and she sagged back against the edge of the sofa with a ragged sigh. They had ended up in each other's arms before because of her compassion, and she couldn't afford another night like that. Besides, this time it would be her walking away, and she got the distinct feeling he would follow her, if only for answers. Her hand slid to her tummy and cradled the scar protectively.

'Do you want a coffee?' she said eventually.

'No, thank you. I'll go now. Thanks for listening.'

As he passed her, she caught his hand and pressed it to her lips, and he turned it to cup her cheek.

'Goodnight, Jo. God bless.'

'Goodnight, Alex.'

She listened to the sound of the front door clicking shut behind him, and thought there was probably no more lonely sound in the world.

Things between them were different after that. Alex seemed freed of his burden and actually began to smile more often, and occasionally he even flirted openly with Jo.

Jo, on the other hand, now knew beyond any doubt that what Alex wanted was a wife and children. If she hadn't realised it from what he had said about his wife, then the fact that he was buying a house with five bedrooms should have alerted her.

But the most significant pointer was the content of his flirting. Every time he caught her looking wistfully at a baby or misty-eyed after a delivery, he would tease her gently and offer to oblige if she ever changed her mind.

It served to strengthen her resolve, and she tried to distance him, but he would have none of it. Almost as if telling her about Cathy had meant he could leave his past behind him, his every action indicated that he was ready now for the future—and that he wanted it to include Jo.

Then there was the infertility clinic. Jo found it very hard going, but she was very good with the patients and it didn't go unnoticed.

Alex stopped her one evening as they were finishing off and called her into his consulting-room.

'I gather you've been talking to the Lucases.'

She nodded. Theirs was a pathetic story of medical

incompetence leading to her sterility because of
blocked Fallopian tubes. IVF had failed repeatedly,
and they were desolate. They desperately wanted a
child, and had wanted to talk about the possibility of
using a surrogate mother, implanted with their own
child. Jo, who had considered the issues of surrogacy
in depth herself, was able to go through the intricacies
of the argument in minute detail, pointing out factors
that they had probably never considered.

'Yes, I tried to help them wade through the pros and
cons.'

'They said you had remarkable insight.'

Jo looked away. 'It's very topical.'

'And you're very alert to human problems and
feelings.' He reached out and touched her hair. 'You'd
be a wonderful mother, Jo. When I see some of the
women who are out there raising children, I think it's
a tragedy that you're denying your potential children
the right to your love and understanding.'

'Oh, God, Alex, not again——'

'Jo. . .' He took her hand and turned her to face
him. 'Look at me.'

With a massive effort of will she drew in a deep
breath and tilted her head back slightly.

His voice was soft, and husky, and wove a spell
around her with its silver threads.

'When I was young, I had a dream. I dreamed that
one day I would be married to a beautiful woman and
have a house full of children, and then grandchildren,
and I'd watch my wife grow old beside me.' His finger
traced the line of her cheek. 'I love you. I want to be
with you, and buy that house, and fill it with the

laughter of our children. Marry me, Jo. Help me make my dream come true.'

Jo stared at him speechlessly.

'Please?'

'Alex, I can't——'

'Why? It's what you want too. Why is your career so important? You're empty, Jo. Let me fill you. . .'

Her throat ached with the effort of holding down the tears, and the yearning grew inside until she felt she would die.

'Oh, Alex, please,' she whispered, 'don't be so cruel. I can't! You don't know how tempting it is—please don't ask me that. Please?'

His eyes searched hers, the warm brown soft with confusion and need. 'Think about it. I'm not going anywhere, Jo. Take your time.'

He released her and moved away, and Jo flexed her fingers. They still burned with the touch of his hand.

'I—I have to go. I'm going out tonight.'

He seemed to withdraw into himself.

'Anywhere nice?'

For a moment she considered letting him think she was going out with another man, but then her innate sense of honesty and integrity came to the fore.

'Supper with Anne Gabriel and Maggie Wells.'

He nodded and seemed to relax slightly. 'Have a lovely time.'

With his proposal echoing in her ears? Fat chance. 'Thank you,' she murmured, and left him there, alone on the edge of the desk, dealing with her rejection.

Anne and Maggie took one look at her and wheedled the whole story out of her. They were understanding

and supportive, but both of them thought she should
tell him about her hysterectomy.

'It isn't fair to him,' Maggie pointed out gently. 'If
he really loves you, you should give him the chance to
prove it——'

'But that's exactly it!' she cried. 'What he'll do,
because he's a gentleman, is say it doesn't make any
difference and of course he still wants to marry me,
and then where will I be? Married to a man who's
desperate for what I can't give him, and after a while
he'll start to hate me, and I couldn't cope with him
hating me. . .'

She pressed her knuckles hard against her lips to
trap the sobs, and Anne cleared the table and Maggie
put the kettle on and started the washing up to give her
time to get a grip on herself.

After a moment or two she stood up and picked up
her jacket.

'I'm rotten company. I think I'll go home.'

'And mope? No way. Anyway, we want to play
cards, so you can't. Open that other bottle of wine and
go and sit down.'

She gave in. She didn't really want to go home and
mope on her own, anyway, so she stayed and cheated
at cards and got rather drunk and slept on the settee,
waking in the morning with a stiff neck and a sore
head.

She went home, showered and changed, and arrived
at the hospital almost human to find Alex out of his
mind with worry.

'Where were you?' he rasped, dragging her into the
sluice.

'At Anne's. I told you I was going out——'

'I tried ringing you—I tried every fifteen minutes until nearly three, then I remembered your house wasn't detached and your neighbours would be getting agitated, so I stopped until six, then tried again. You didn't say you were going to be out for the night!' he added accusingly.

'Alex, since when were you my keeper?' she asked him angrily.

'It's not a case of being your keeper—I love you, damn it! I was worried!'

A nurse came in, stopped in her tracks and went away again, trying unsuccessfully to hide her smile.

Jo groaned. 'Do we have to have this conversation in public?' she asked him.

He glanced round, collected himself and apologised.

'Why were you trying to ring me anyway?'

'The survey—the report came in the post. I found it when I got home. The house is fine, bar needing a lot of work, but nothing nasty. It's been rewired and replumbed in the past, and the roof's sound.'

She swallowed. 'So will you buy it?'

'Yes—and live in hope.'

'Oh, Alex, forget about me! If you want it, buy it, but don't drag me into it, please!'

They were interrupted yet again, this time by the sister.

'I've got a nurse hovering out here with a bedpan—perhaps you could move your argument elsewhere?' she said with a smile.

'Sorry, Sister,' Alex said with a rueful grin, and escorted Jo out into the corridor. The nurse watched them go with fascinated interest.

Jo's heart sank. It would be all over the hospital in minutes.

She missed lunch as she was in Theatre with a tricky forceps delivery, and by the time she made her way to the canteen it was almost deserted. She collected a salad and went over by the window, staring out and wondering where Alex was.

Someone came in, and her ears picked up the slightly uneven gait. She turned with a smile and watched as the tall, blond man in theatre greens with an almost imperceptible limp made his way over to her.

'Michael—how's things?'

He grinned. 'Never better. Mind if I join you?'

'Of course not.' She moved her tray out of his way and watched as he sat down and grimaced.

'Leg hurting you?'

'I've been on it a lot. Still, I should get my new state-of-the-art American leg soon, so perhaps it will be better.'

Jo grinned. 'If it gets much better, Clare will have to watch out, you old lady-killer!'

He chuckled, but his eyes were tender. 'I'd never do that to her, you know that.'

'Yes, I know. Give yourself time, Michael—you only lost the damn thing in June.'

'Not you, too! I get this all day from Clare.' He shifted his plate off the tray and picked up his fork. 'So, what's this I hear about you slaying the boss?' he mumbled through a mouthful of food.

Jo groaned. 'The tom-toms been at it again?'

Michael chuckled. 'Why should you be any different? So, tell all—is this the big romance of your life?'

Something must have shown in her eyes, because he

stretched out a hand and covered hers as they lay twisted together on the table.

'Want to talk about it?'

'It won't change anything, but I know you'll understand. He wants to marry me, and have scads of kids.'

He watched her closely. 'And is that a problem?'

'Yes, it's a problem.' She turned her hands over and clung to him. 'Michael, I can't have children.'

His face showed first disbelief, then shock, then understanding. He squeezed her hands, and put down his fork, and swore, softly and explicitly.

'Exactly.'

'Oh, hell, Jo, I'm sorry. So what will you do?'

'What can I do? Pray for a career move and get away from him.'

'Run away, you mean.'

'Do I?'

He nodded slowly. 'I think so. Jo, you ought to tell him. He deserves a chance to make up his own mind.'

'Not you, too! He'll marry me out of pity——'

'That's what I said about Clare, but she married me, and, believe me, she married me for love. Nothing else would have been strong enough to cope with my temper in the past few months.'

Jo smiled weakly. 'I'm glad for you, but it's different. Children are somehow intrinsic—Michael, I've been working with the couples in the infertility clinic, and some of their marriages are on the brink because they can't have children.'

'Yes, but you would know in advance, so it would be different. Your marriage would be based on different assumptions and different choices. I think you should give him the opportunity to discuss it with you. You never know, you might be surprised.'

She shook her head. 'No, I don't think so. I know how he feels about children. And have you noticed how everybody's pregnant? Lizzi Hamilton's due in February, Bron Henderson is due in April——'

'Clare's due in May.'

Jo lifted her head and stared at him for an age, then swallowed the lump in her throat. 'Oh, Michael, that's great news!'

'Is it?' He gave a hollow laugh. 'At first I thought it was an unmitigated disaster. I'm only just coming to terms with it now.'

She smiled, genuinely pleased for him. 'It'll be a beautiful baby, with all those good-looking genes. How's Clare?'

'Sick. She's really finding it rough going this week.'

'Tell her to take time off. Talking of which, I have to go back to work.'

She stood up, and Michael reached out a hand and caught her wrist. 'Jo, give him a chance. Give yourself a chance. Maybe you need each other more than you need children.'

'I'll think about it,' she promised him, and she did think about it, almost to the exclusion of anything else, for the next week and a half.

Then on Friday afternoon as she came out of Theatre Alex cornered her.

'Hi. Are you busy tonight?'

'Not so you'd notice—why?'

'I've got the keys of the house—the solicitor rang me at lunchtime to tell me the deal was completed and the house is mine. I wondered if you would like to come over and look round and help me with decisions about carpets and curtains and suchlike. I'm not very good in that department.'

She was terribly torn. Part of her loved homemaking and would like nothing more, and the other part of her flinched from any further painful contact with Alex. Because he would work on her, she realised that. He might be quiet and conservative and subdued, but he was also relentless, and he wanted her.

'What makes you think I'm any good?' she asked, stalling for time.

'Your cottage is lovely. You've got a definite knack. Please? I'd hate to make an expensive mistake.'

She was defeated. 'What time?' she asked wearily.

'Are you ready now?'

She glanced at her watch. 'I'll have to take my bleep and come back later to check my patients.'

'That's OK. I have to come back too. We can leave your car here.'

They spent half an hour in an interiors shop borrowing carpet and fabric samples, and then went to the house.

After some friendly bickering that proved Alex to be quite capable of making up his own mind, he sat back and said, 'Why don't you just tell me what you'd like, and I'll listen, and anything I like I'll pick up on. Otherwise it's just going to be compromise, and that never works.'

So she outlined her suggestions, and he noted down colourways and names and manufacturers, then dragged her into the kitchen.

'What about in here? What would you do?'

'Budget?'

He shrugged. 'Whatever's necessary—several thousand, I imagine.'

'OK.' She looked round, and chewed her lip. 'Right, I'd leave the sink there under the front window, and build a peninsular unit out to divide the room and give more work area, and leave this end as a breakfast area overlooking the garden.'

'Like a family-room?' he suggested, and she looked away.

'If you like,' she said tightly, and he sighed and apologised.

'Forget that. I wasn't trying to put pressure on you.'

She shook her head helplessly. 'It doesn't matter.'

'What about the units?'

'What?'

'The kitchen units—wood, paint finish, laminate?'

'Oh. Light oak or beech, to go with the panelling in the hall, I think. Perhaps dark green worktops—that's very smart with the light oak and would carry the hall carpet through.'

He was jotting. 'Flooring?'

'Ceramic tiles in the kitchen area, or maybe sheet flooring for comfort. If it was me I'd go for ceramic tiles because of my heels—they dig holes in wood or vinyl. And carry the hall carpet through to the breakfast area.'

'Built-in oven, hob, fridge, freezer, dishwasher?'

'Uh-huh—and microwave. Put the washing-machine and tumble-drier in the utility-room with the same units.'

'Tiled floor?'

'Makes sense, straight out of the garden.'

'Great.' He slapped the notebook shut. 'Back to the

hospital, and then dinner—how about a take-away at
your house while we look at the curtain fabrics?'

'What?'

He shruged innocently. 'I want to get it all under
way. I can order everything tomorrow morning, and
then it can be ready as soon as possible.'

'What about the upstairs?'

He was hustling her towards the door. 'Too dark
now. We'll do that another day. Perhaps we can choose
the carpets tonight at your house. Give me a hand with
this lot.'

He hoisted the samples up and dumped them in Jo's
arms, then picked up the carpet books and ushered her
out.

'This better be a damn good take-away,' she said.

'The best. Come on.'

'I must be nuts,' she muttered, but she followed him
anyway. He was so preoccupied with the house that he
seemed likely to leave her alone.

As she settled herself into the car, a bleep went.

'Yours or mine?' he asked, picking up the car phone
and punching in the hospital number.

'Yours.'

'Alexander Carter—you bleeped me. Thank you.'

He turned to her with a grimace. 'Hopefully this
won't take long—hello? Yes, Sister. OK, I'm on my
way in. Admit her while you're waiting.'

He put the phone down and started the car. 'One of
the staff nurses from another department is threatening
to abort. I suppose they called me because it's staff.'

'Do you mind?'

'Of course not, but she might prefer you.'

'I'll come with you. You might need someone to assist.'

He flashed her one of his rare smiles. 'I'd be grateful.'

Jo's heart turned over. She thought then that she'd do almost anything for one of those beautiful smiles.

CHAPTER SIX

THEY turned into the hospital car park a few minutes later, and made their way quickly to the ward.

As they walked through the door, Jo caught a glimpse of a familiar green-clad back bending over a bed in a side-ward. She pulled Alex to a halt and stuck her head round the door.

'Michael?'

He lifted his head, his eyes worried, and his face flooded with relief. 'Oh, Jo, thank God you're here. Clare fainted on the ward about an hour ago, but she wouldn't go home. Mary O'Brien called me out of Theatre and got me to bring her up here. Now she's bleeding.'

His voice was taut with anxiety, and Jo squeezed his hand and plastered a reassuring smile on her face. Michael might be pleased to see her, but she was probably the last person in the world Clare wanted to see. In the weeks after Michael's accident she had provided him with a shoulder to cry on, and Clare had been sure that they were having an affair. Jo still wasn't sure if she was really convinced of their innocence.

Still, all that was water under the bridge. Her job now was to reassure, assess and render appropriate medical assistance. Anything else could wait. Alex had already moved to the basin in the corner and was scrubbing his hands, and a nurse appeared with a trolley equipped for examinations.

101

'I'll tell Sister you're here,' she said, and left the room.

Jo laid a hand on Clare's wrist and felt her pulse. It was slightly fast, but steady.

'Hello, Clare. How are you feeling now?'

'Rotten—I've been feeling awful for days.'

Jo nodded. 'We need to have a look at you—this is Alex Carter, the consultant.'

Alex gave Clare a slight smile and eased back the bedclothes. 'Let's see what we can find. When was your last period?'

'Fourth of August,' Michael said promptly.

Alex raised one eyebrow. 'So you're about seven or eight weeks pregnant, right?'

'Eight on Monday,' Clare told him. 'I've been feeling very pregnant right from the beginning.'

Alex nodded, his hands firm but gentle as he palpated her abdomen. As he pressed down on one side, Clare winced.

'Sorry,' he murmured. 'That's a bit tender, isn't it? Have you had an internal examination since you were admitted?'

'No.'

'OK. I'll do one now. What colour is the blood you're losing?'

'Dark,' she said quietly. 'There's not a lot. . .'

'Don't worry.' His hand closed over hers and squeezed gently. 'We'll sort you out.'

After the internal, during which Michael sat with his eyes glued on Clare's face and his hands gripping hers tightly, Alex pulled off his gloves, covered her up and sighed.

'Well?' Michael asked shortly.

'Well, I think we need to get a scan done. It could be one of several things, or a combination. It could be an ovarian cyst—the blood loss is very slight, isn't it? That could easily be because your second period is due about now. It could be a pelvic infection, although you don't seem to have a high temperature. There's a slight possibility it could be due to an ectopic pregnancy, or it could be just a very slight, threatened miscarriage which could go either way. A scan will help to define the problem.'

He went to the door and held it open, indicating that Jo should go with him.

'See you in a minute,' she said to Michael and Clare, and went out into the corridor with Alex.

As soon as the door was closed she dragged him up the corridor out of earshot and turned to face him.

'You have to get her into Theatre now,' she said urgently.

'What? Calm down, Jo. There's time——'

'Not if it's an ectopic about to rupture!'

He regarded her thoughtfully. 'And if we hustle her in there and open her up and it's a threatened abortion that might have settled down left alone? What then?'

She took a deep breath. 'Alex, I'm sure she's got an ectopic pregnancy. She's in a hell of a lot of pain in the left iliac fossa.'

'She didn't seem that bad——'

'You weren't looking at her eyes.'

He folded his arms and leant against the wall. 'I thought you were all for letting things take their course and avoiding intervention unless it's absolutely essential?'

'You're talking about two entirely different things!'

she argued. 'This is hardly in the same league as a forceps delivery! All the signs point to it——'

'They point to all sorts of possible things at the moment——'

'Alex, listen to me, *please*! I *know* she's got an ectopic!'

'Well, I don't. I don't know any such thing, and until I'm more certain I'm not prepared to take any action, particularly not based on your intuition.'

Jo was beyond reason.

'Alex, you have to do something before it ruptures!' she pleaded.

He studied her seriously. 'You really mean it, don't you?'

She shrugged helplessly. 'Call it intuition, call it what you like. I'd stake my professional reputation on it.'

He sighed. 'OK. We'll alert Theatre, prep her up and do a scan while we wait. All right?'

She flashed him a smile. 'Thanks. I'll sort out the ultrasound.' She went down to Sister's office, rang the ultrasound technician on duty and asked her to bring the portable ultrasound up to the ward, and went back to Clare's room.

By the time she arrived Alex had alerted Theatre and was explaining to Clare and Michael what they were proposing to do. When he had finished, he went to phone the anaesthetist while a nurse shaved her. Michael was standing by the window rubbing his left thigh absently and staring into space. She smiled at him reassuringly, and he closed his eyes and swallowed hard.

Then the anaesthetist arrived, and Jo led Michael

out of the room, ostensibly to give everyone room to do their job.

'I thought I didn't want it,' he said with a humourless laugh. 'Now I feel as if my thoughts have damned my own child.'

'Don't be melodramatic,' Jo said mildly. 'Have a toffee.'

He unwrapped it mechanically and chewed for a second or two before his eyes found Jo's again.

'She will be all right, won't she?'

'Michael, you're a doctor. You know perfectly well what the risks are. Yes, of course she'll be all right.'

'It's an ectopic, isn't it?'

She was silent for a moment, then she nodded. 'I think so.'

'And Alex?'

'He's hedging his bets,' she said with a little smile.

'But he's going along with you.'

She shrugged. 'Perhaps he has faith in my clinical judgment.'

Michael watched her closely. 'And you don't have faith in his?'

'Of course I do. He's just slower to jump to conclusions than I am. I tend to rely on gut instinct—not always correctly! Don't worry, he won't open her up without a good reason, but he's getting ready to do it earlier on my say so.'

'Why are you so sure——? Oh, God.' His eyes tracked slowly over her face, understanding dawning as he read her expression. 'Is that what happened to you?'

Jo nodded.

'But you said——'

'It's quite different. I had a congenital problem——'

'With what?'

Alex was standing right behind her.

'My brain. That's why I'm so good at diagnosing the invisible—second sight. How is she?' Dear God, what had he heard?

'Iffy. The pain is getting worse. We'll take her up now.'

'What about the scan?' Jo asked.

'Forget it. I don't want to wait.'

'Can I come into Theatre?'

They both turned and looked at Michael, then at each other.

'Only if you promise not to faint,' Alex said.

He grinned. 'Fair dos. She watched them amputate my leg.'

Alex blinked.

'Haven't you heard about me? They call me the Bionic Man.'

Jo laughed. 'Come on, let's get Clare up to Theatre and sort her out.'

It was a simple operation, but Alex worked fast and very, very carefully. If it was an ectopic pregnancy, the slightest sudden movement or untoward pressure could rupture it and cause a massive haemorrhage.

As Jo watched his hands and held the retractors for him, she was assailed by doubts. What if she was wrong? What if she was putting Clare through this unnecessarily?

'Keep still, woman, you're jiggling all over the place,' Alex snapped, and she forced herself to calm down. Better safe than sorry, she told herself, but her doubts were unfounded. The left Fallopian tube, hugely distended by the embedded embryo, was on the point of rupture when they reached it, and Alex clamped the blood vessels immediately and then excised the damaged portion.

'Well, we got that in the nick of time, thanks to Jo's intuition,' he said with a sigh, and his eyes met Michael's over his mask. 'Sorry, old man.'

Michael swallowed hard and gave a wry grin. 'It probably won't hurt us to have a bit of time alone together.'

Alex nodded. 'I've taken out that bit of the tube, but it all looks healthy otherwise. Joining the ends just makes it more likely that she'll have another ectopic in the future, but the potential is there if anything should happen to the other side. Perhaps it was just a minor glitch in that tube—a narrowing of the isthmus for some reason.'

Michael was taking an avid interest. 'It all looks healthy enough. I wonder what caused it?'

'Who knows?' Alex shrugged, and sutured the wound with elaborate care. 'There, she'll soon be good as new, but give her a few months—six or so—before you try again.'

Michael snorted with laughter. 'Six months? You jest! More like six years!'

'Don't bargain on tomorrow,' Alex said quietly. 'It doesn't always come. OK, thank you, everybody. You can take her through to Recovery now. Are you going to stay with her?'

'If I may?' Michael said. He looked thoughtful.

'Of course. Excuse us, we have a date with a Chinese take-away.'

Alex put his hand in the small of Jo's back and propelled her through the door.

'Who said anything about Chinese?'

'OK, Indian——'

'Or Indian?'

Alex sighed in exasperation as they stripped off their soiled gowns and dumped them in the bin. 'What do you want? Greek? Italian?'

'Fish and chips.'

'Fish and. . .? OK. We'll have fish and chips. See you outside in two minutes.'

She took five, mainly because she was still reeling from the shock of Clare's operation. It was all a little too close to home, but at least Clare hadn't ruptured. Given time, she would be almost as good as new.

Unlike me, she thought heavily. . .

'What are you doing in there, going to sleep?'

'Bully. I'm coming.'

She dragged on her dress, raked a comb over her hair and joined him outside Theatre.

By the time they got back to her house it was late, and they were content to sit and eat the food out of the paper at the kitchen table. As he finished, Alex crumpled up his paper and sat back with a contented sigh.

'Fantastic. Now, about fabric——'

Jo groaned.

'No?'

'Not tonight, Alex. I'm tired.'

'Me, too. How about a cup of coffee and a cuddle on the sofa?'

Abandoning the remains of her meal, she stood up

and moved away from the mute appeal of his warm brown eyes. 'How about a cup of coffee?'

He sighed and laughed and shook his head. 'It was worth a try. Coffee would be lovely, thanks. Can I help?'

'Make one cup of instant coffee? I think I can manage.'

'I could have tea with you, if you like.'

'It's better for you. I'll make it; you go and find a CD and put it on.'

By the time she joined him, a Mozart horn concerto was filling the sitting-room, drowning out their conversation. She sat in the chair, and he gave her a reproachful look and settled on one end of the settee.

'This is the best seat,' she told him in a lull, 'because the speakers are arranged for it.'

'How generous of you to offer to share it,' he said, trying not to laugh, and in a flash she was hoisted up into the air and was settled on his lap.

She squirmed, and he drew in a sharp breath and held her still.

'Don't wriggle about. I'm already half out of my mind for you.'

She froze, and he laughed softly and hugged her. 'Relax, you're quite safe,' he said reassuringly.

She felt safe—that wasn't the problem! But she found it surprisingly easy to relax against him and let the music flow around them. It reminded her of Alex—crisp and precise and nothing excessively emotional or sentimental, but disturbing nevertheless.

The concerto came to an end, but neither of them moved. Alex's hand was resting lightly on her thigh, and the warmth seemed to radiate out from it, wrapping her in a cocoon.

His other hand drew lazy circles on her back, and she felt his touch right through to her bones. She was conscious of his mouth just inches from her own, and when he turned his head she moved instinctively closer to meet his lips.

His kissed her slowly, almost tentatively, and then pulled away and tucked her head into the curve of his shoulder.

'Did I say well done for spotting that ectopic?' he murmured, and her sanity seeped back like cold water.

'It was nothing,' she mumbled.

'It wasn't nothing, it was an inspired piece of diagnostic skill. Perhaps you're right—you should have got my job. I would probably have let her rupture, but her symptoms just weren't that severe.'

'They often aren't with ectopics,' Jo said, 'especially a first. It's easy to ignore the niggles until it's too late.'

'Hmm. Where were we?' He tilted her chin towards him, but she turned her head.

'It's late, Alex.'

He sighed. 'Do you want me to go?'

No! her body screamed. Stay and make love to me, and tell me you love me and it doesn't matter, and make me believe it. . .

'Yes, please, Alex.'

'What about the samples?'

She struggled to her feet and rubbed her hand tiredly over her eyes.

'Another day, maybe.'

He nodded and stood up. 'OK. Sleep well. I'll see you tomorrow—who's on call tonight?'

She smiled slowly. 'I believe you are.'

He gave a reluctant laugh. 'Oh, well, it's as effective as a cold shower, I suppose. Bye, love.' He dropped a kiss on her cheek and let himself out.

Clare was still groggy in the morning, but she smiled wanly at Jo when she went in.

'Hi. How are you today?'

'Sore—my throat as well from the airway. I've never had an operation. Perhaps it'll make me a better nurse.'

Jo chuckled. 'Probably, although judging by what I hear from Michael you're a very good one already.'

Clare blushed, and Jo went on, 'He also reckons you're going to be a rotten patient.'

She snorted. 'Him—he's got no room to talk. He's the world's worst patient.'

'I believe it!' Jo said with a laugh. Then the smile faded from her lips and she looked out of the window. 'Clare, I'm sorry about the baby.'

There was silence for a moment.

'Yes, well, we can't have everything. The timing wasn't exactly great—with all the problems we've had so far, we could do with time to get to know each other better before we introduce another variable.'

Jo perched on the edge of the bed. 'Clare, about me and Michael—you do believe there was nothing between us, don't you?'

She smiled weakly. 'I do now—I didn't then, because you're so damn lovely and Michael's—well, he——'

'Sexy as sin? I know that. I also know he's head over heels in love with you, and, if I hadn't noticed, by the end of the first week of him crying on my shoulder it might have registered! And how can you lie there and talk about my looks as if they were a threat? Have you looked in a mirror in the past twenty years?'

Clare giggled and clutched her abdomen. 'Oh—rats, I hate not being able to laugh.'

Jo patted her hand. 'I'm glad you feel you want to. Has Michael been up to see you yet?'

'He's been here all night, apparently, sleeping in the chair. He won't leave me.'

Jo forced a smile. What she wouldn't have done for Alex's solid presence supporting her through her post-op misery.

'He's a lovely man, and you're both very lucky to have each other. You take care of him.'

She left Clare, and busied herself with the overnight admissions. By the look of it Alex hadn't needed his cold shower. He must have been rushed off his feet.

It was a fairly quiet weekend after that, and Jo spent some time in her little garden hauling up weeds and trimming back perennials ready for the winter. October had come in, cold and damp, and the winter stretched away ahead of her bleakly. Perhaps she would find a hobby inside, like patchwork or cross-stitch or something creative like that—something to take away the emptiness of the long, cold hours alone.

The next couple of weeks were busy as usual, but that suited Jo. She had plenty to do without moping for Alex, and in fact they were both so busy with their own lists that they hardly ever met.

Clare went home to stay with her mother as Michael couldn't afford any more time off, and Jo fed him on occasions and watched with quiet sympathy as he dealt with his feelings about the baby.

'Ridiculous, isn't it? I mean, we didn't even want it,' he said on one such occasion. It was the Friday night two weeks after her operation, and Jo let him get drunk and sleep on her sofa. In the morning she roused him, ran him a bath and made him eat breakfast before sending him off to fetch Clare, who was coming home that day.

She went into the hospital and found Alex broody and uncommunicative. The third time he snapped at her for no good reason, she followed him into the ward office.

'Did I do something?' she asked him bluntly.

'I don't know, did you?'

'What?'

He glared at her. 'Barrington's car was outside your house all night.'

She straightened her shoulders and turned to look out of the window over the ward. How the hell did he know that? Not that there was any point in denying it. She had nothing to hide.

'Yes—yes, it was. What has that got to do with your temper?'

'Damn it, woman, what the hell do you think?'

'Are you spying on me?' she asked with deadly quiet.

He exhaled sharply. 'You know what this place is like—rumour's rife. The least you could have done is gone to his place where your car wouldn't be noticed!'

She turned to face him. 'Do I take it that you've been listening to these rumours?'

He glared at her. 'What the hell am I supposed to think? Damn it, you had an affair just before he got married. Everyone thought it was patched up, but evidently it wasn't. How convenient that Clare was immobilised and sent away!'

She didn't think. Her hand flew up and caught him across his cheek with the full weight of her arm behind it, and then she turned on her heel, stalked out of the ward and went down to the car park. Let him deal with the patients on his own.

She drove home and attacked her garden again, and ignored the insistent ringing of the phone.

At five she straightened up, the cold and the drizzle finally defeating her, and saw Alex standing by her back door, watching her.

She brushed past him, stripped off her gloves and washed her hands at the kitchen sink.

'How did you get in?'

'The door was unlocked. You should be more careful.'

She snorted. 'That's obvious—all sorts of scum could walk in off the street.'

'Jo, listen——'

'No, you listen to me!' She whirled round, her eyes blazing. 'I don't care what you or anyone else thinks about me, but I resent the fact that in your position you listen to idle gossip about your colleagues and encourage the tittle-tattling that goes on! Clare's and Michael's relationship was nearly wrecked by it before, and I'm damned if I'm going to stand by and let it happen again! What I want to know is, how do they know his car was here? Hardly anybody knows where I live——'

'I do.'

'What?' She floundered to a halt.

'They weren't gossiping about his car. As far as I

know, I'm the only one who saw it. I came to see you last night, but his car was here. I came back later, and it was still here. When I went home from the hospital at four, it was here, and when I went back in at nine——'

'He was just about sober enough to get in it and drive to Cambridge to collect Clare from her parents.'

'What?' It was his turn to look puzzled.

Jo sighed and put the kettle on. There was no point in this stupid argument.

'He was drunk when he arrived, and he brought a bottle of wine and sat down and worked his way steadily through it while he rambled on about Clare and the baby and life and his leg and medicine in general and Clare in particular. He wasn't fit to drive home, so when he finally drifted off on the sofa I covered him up with a blanket and left him to it. Even if I'd wanted to sleep with him he would have been totally incapable.'

'And did you?'

She gave a heavy sigh. 'No, I didn't—nor have I, at any time. He's just a friend, and last night he needed a shoulder to cry on.'

Alex met her eyes, his own still racked with doubt. 'Four years ago I needed a shoulder to cry on—I seem to remember you were most obliging.'

Jo felt the blood drain from her face. 'Bastard!' she whispered. 'That was different and you know it.'

His eyes fell, and to her surprise he flushed a dull red.

'I'm sorry. You're right, it was different.' He lifted his head, and his eyes were filled with remorse. 'Forgive me—I had no right to make those accusations. I was sitting in the canteen in the middle of the night and I overheard two junior nurses gossiping. You'd apparently been seen together rather a lot this past week. I nearly went berserk. Then when I went past his car was still here—I was ready to kill you by this morning.'

She reached out her hand to touch him, and thought better of it. Instead she made a pot of tea and found some chocolate biscuits in a cupboard. She poured the tea, plonked it on the table and sat down, dunking her biscuit in the hot tea and licking off the chocolate.

'That's disgusting,' he said with a mock shudder.

'It's my only vice,' she told him with studied emphasis, and dunked again. 'Try it.'

'God, no,' he said with apparent distaste, but he watched her hungrily.

'So,' she mumbled, wiping soggy crumbs off her chin, 'what did you want me for?'

He choked on his tea. When he finished coughing, he wiped his eyes on his handkerchief and cleared his throat. 'Pardon?'

She kept the smile from her lips. 'Last night—you came to see me. Why?'

He shrugged. 'I had something to show you—it doesn't matter.'

'You should have come in.'

'I didn't dare. I didn't know what I'd find.'

She covered his hand and he turned it palm up and gripped her fingers.

'I'm sorry you were worried.'

'I wasn't worried, exactly. Jealous, perhaps?'

'There was no need.'

'I know.'

'Do you?'

He lifted her hand and pressed a kiss on her palm that sent shivers down her spine. 'Yes, I know. I do now, anyway. I'm sorry I got heavy.'

He stood up, put his mug in the sink and headed for the door. Jo followed him.

'So what was it that you wanted to show me?'

He looked away, and she had the craziest feeling he was unsure of himself.

'It's at the house.'

'Can I come over this evening? I'm on call tonight, but early evening should be all right.'

'Seven? I'll feed you.'

'OK. I'll drive myself in case I have to go to the hospital. And Alex?' She stopped him with a hand on his arm, and he turned towards her, his face carefully masked.

'Yes?'

'Thank you for coming round.'

He smiled slowly, and her heart rose in her throat. 'I just wanted to make sure it was safe to go back into the hospital without being beaten up.'

She laughed, a low, delighted ripple of sound.

'God, you've got a sexy laugh,' he murmured, and pulled her into his arms, kissing her soundly before letting himself out. 'See you later,' he murmured huskily, and then he was gone, and she wondered why she'd been so willing to assure him he had no reason to be jealous of Michael, when she should have been telling him he had no reason to be jealous, full stop, because her social life was none of his business.

The trouble was, she wanted it to be his business,

she acknowledged with a sigh as she went up to the
bedroom and stripped ready for her bath.

And crazy though it was, she was secretly delighted
that he was jealous.

CHAPTER SEVEN

JO ARRIVED at the house at seven exactly, and as she approached security lights came on and lit her way to the door. After she rang the doorbell, she glanced around with interest. It looked as if someone had been busy in the front garden, tidying up the neglected beds and rescuing the lawn from the knee-high weeds and grasses. Through the stained-glass window to the left of the front door, lights glowed a welcome, and she found herself wondering if he had got round to ordering any of the things she had suggested, or if he had decided on something different.

She didn't have long to wait. Within moments the door was opened and Alex, dressed in casual trousers and a roll-neck lambswool sweater, smiled a somewhat diffident welcome. Oh, that smile! She longed to lift her hand and touch the corner of his mouth, longed to pull his head down and kiss those firm, well-sculptured lips. She ached to hold him, to feel the solid strength of his body in her arms——

'Are you coming in?' he asked, and, pulling herself together, she stepped numbly through the doorway—on to carpet.

Surprised, she looked blankly round.

It was changed almost beyond recognition. The hall panelling was gleaming with polish, the wood lustrous and rich, and on the floor was a thick, soft, heathery

green carpet that ran through into the sitting-room and
dining-room.

'You've done it!' she said in awed astonishment.
'You've done everything we talked about. . .'

She wandered into the sitting-room. Hanging at the
windows were long floral curtains in a heavy satin, with
matching pelmets in the style she had sketched on the
back of an old envelope. A large, comfortable suite of
two two-seaters and two chairs was drawn up round
the fireplace, and here and there were nice little tables,
obviously old and valuable, and in the centre of the
group a lovely washed Chinese rug in soft peaches and
greens tied in with the curtains. The walls were colour-
washed in delicate bluey-greens, and a few carefully-
placed table-lamps cast a warm glow round the cosy
room.

Numbly she went through into the dining-room and
noted the Georgian mahogany table, the elegant chairs,
the formal striped curtains with swagged pelmet.

The kitchen was unfinished, but the units were oak
and matched the hall panelling almost exactly. A
peninsular unit projected into the room, and there
were holes in the cabinets where the appliances would
fit. There was a roll of green carpet on the floor ready
to go down at the other end when the kitchen was
finished, but the kitchen area was tiled in warm terra-
cotta Spanish tiles. Dark green worktops in plastic
sheeting lay at the other end, waiting to be fitted.

Jo swallowed. It was all turning out exactly as she
had envisaged it, and she could hardly bear to look.

'Come and see upstairs,' Alex urged, taking her
elbow.

She allowed him to lead her up the broad staircase

and into the master bedroom. She hadn't seen the scheme for this room, because Clare's operation had intervened on that evening, but she loved it anyway. The carpet was a soft old rose, and the curtains were very traditional, huge roses in delicate hues tumbling in profusion over the windows. There was a vast bed in the middle of the wall opposite the window, and she noticed through the doorway into the dressing-room that a white bathroom suite was wrapped and standing in the room, waiting to be installed.

The two other double rooms were similarly decorated, but the little rooms were untouched.

'I thought I'd let you decide what you wanted to do with them,' Alex said quietly.

'Me?' She looked at him in puzzled surprise. 'Why me?'

'I just thought you'd like to,' he said with a shrug.

Her heart started to hammer, and she felt fear rising like bile in her throat.

She turned away and went back into the master bedroom, moving the curtain aside to stare out into the dark night.

'So, what do you think? Do you like it?'

She found her voice. 'It's worked very well; I think you should be very pleased. You must have moved heaven and earth to get it done so quickly.'

He laughed, and she thought she noticed a touch of relief. 'Let's just say I greased a few palms. Do you like this room? I didn't know what you'd want, but I saw this fabric and it just seemed you——'

'Why, Alex?'

'What?'

She was calm, composed, although her nerves felt shredded. 'Why should it matter what I want?'

Alex sighed and ran his hand through his hair. 'I should have thought that was obvious, Jo.'

'Not to me it isn't—perhaps you'd better spell it out.'

He sat heavily on the edge of the bed and leant his elbows on his knees.

'I thought, maybe, just possibly, the house might tempt you to change your mind. I was obviously wrong. I'm sorry.'

His simple honesty wrung her heart. 'Oh, Alex, I'm sorry too. It's a lovely house. I'd be very happy to share it with you, but I can't.'

'You could, if you weren't so damn stubborn!' he said grimly. 'If you didn't have this fixed idea that you couldn't mix marriage and work together, we could have all this, and more, but oh, no, it's got to be one or the other!'

His voice was rising to a shout, and he pushed himself to his feet, pacing round the room like an angry tiger.

'Why, damn it? We could have so much together. Why?'

Jo closed her eyes. The last thing she could tell him was why.

'Because I'm just that kind of woman,' she told him quietly instead, and turned towards the door. 'I think I'd better go——'

'Jo, wait!' His voice was softer now, less angry. She waited, and he crossed the room almost silently on the thick rose-pink carpet and turned her towards him. 'I'm sorry I pushed you—sorry I tried to bribe you. It was just one last-ditch chance that didn't pay off—not that it matters about the house, because I like all of it anyway and I couldn't have done it half so well without your help——' His voice cracked and he closed his eyes.

The room was silent except for the harsh sound of his breathing. She was aware of him as she had never been—the pulse beating in his temple, the thick lashes that hid his eyes from sight, the soft rasp of his thumbs stroking rhythmically on her arms as he held her. For a moment she thought he was going to break down, but then he deliberately slowed his breathing and brought himself under control with a visible effort.

After a moment he went on, with quiet dignity, 'I won't plead or grovel, and I won't make your life hell at work, but I want you to know that I'll go to my grave loving you. I hoped you could love me too—I thought we had something really special. . .'

He opened his eyes and looked at her, and the desolation was back, that awful desolation that made his beautiful brown eyes a wasteland of pain and sorrow.

'Oh, Alex,' she whispered, and the heavy tears welled and slipped down her cheeks. 'I never wanted to hurt you. . .'

She lifted her hand and cupped his cheek, and a ragged sob rose in his chest and tore free. With a massive effort he controlled it and stepped back a fraction.

'Go on, then, if you're going.'

She closed her eyes and pressed her hand to her lips. The tears fell faster, and a tiny sob escaped into the quiet room.

'Ah, love, don't cry. I'll be fine. Don't cry, Jo, please, darling—oh, God!'

With a ragged moan he wrapped his arms around her and crushed her against his chest. She could feel the shudders running through him, and his heart was hammering against her ribs. Tilting back her head, she pressed her lips to his damp cheek, but he turned his head and their lips met and clung.

Instantly fire leapt between them, and his arms slid up her sides until his hands cupped her face, holding her steady while his mouth plundered hers with barely restrained desperation. Her own hands slid down and edged under the soft sweater, her fingers finding warm skin and rippling muscle as they explored his broad back.

His hands locked behind her hips and tugged her hard against him, and she felt the shocking pressure of his arousal as he rocked her against him.

She made a low sound of desire deep in her throat, and before she could move he lifted her and laid her on the bed, coming down beside her and wrapping her in his arms.

He was wild with need, voracious and demanding, and she was frantic to hold him, to touch him, to feel him. . .

Mindlessly she tugged at the sweater and he wrenched it off over his head, hurling it aside as her hands reached up and pulled him back, greedy for the feel of his hot skin against her palms.

Raising himself up on one elbow, he unfastened the buttons down the front of her dress with trembling fingers.

'Damn, I can't. . .' he muttered, and she helped him,

no steadier but just as desperate, until finally the edges fell apart and she lay covered only in the fine silk of her flimsy underwear. He thrust the sides back over her shoulders and bent his head, taking her nipples into his mouth one by one, heedless of the fine satin covering them. The moist satin chaffed and cooled, and her nipples pebbled under his blazing eyes.

'I want to see you,' he groaned, and his fingers sought and found the fastening on the teddy, sliding it up until her body was revealed to his hungry gaze. His lips parted on a harsh breath as he let his eyes trail over her nakedness.

'Dear God, you are exquisite,' he breathed, his trembling fingers tracing an unsteady path from her collar-bone down over her breasts and back up again, making her shudder with need. She dug her nails into his shoulders and pulled him down against her, gasping at the first contact of her sensitive nipples with the coarse hair of his chest.

His mouth found hers and clung, and one hand continued its foray down her body, trailing down her hip and over her thigh, circling frustratingly wide of the mark. She moaned against his lips, writhing against him, and his hand tracked to the soft curls, his long fingers teasing, tormenting.

Mindless with need, she arched against his hand, her fingers restless against his back, urging him on.

'Alex, please!' she begged, and then slowly sanity filtered back as she became aware of his absolute stillness. Her mouth suddenly dry, her body lost its restless striving need and seemed to crumple against the bed. A cold dread consumed her.

'Alex?' she whispered.

He lifted himself up on one elbow and looked down at her body, his fingers tracing the faint line of the scar. She could feel his hand trembling.

'What happened?' he asked, his voice deadly quiet.

Oh, God, how to tell him without implicating him and his child?

'I had a hysterectomy,' she told him, surprised at the steadiness of her voice. 'I was bleeding heavily, and Owen found a deformity that would have precluded having a successful pregnancy. A hysterectomy was the obvious answer.'

It wasn't a lie, precisely, but still she couldn't meet his eyes, and after a few seconds he rolled away from her and sat up on the far side of the bed, his head bowed.

The silence stretched on endlessly, broken eventually by the insistent bleeping of her pager in the hall.

Stiffly, Alex got to his feet and went downstairs, returning with a cordless phone.

'You'd better ring in,' he said, his voice curiously wooden. He looked shattered.

Taking the phone, she punched in the numbers and wished she weren't sitting in the middle of his bed with her clothing in disarray while he stood motionless at the window, staring out. She knelt up and turned her back to him.

The hospital answered, connected her to the ward and she spoke quickly to Anne Gabriel.

'We've got problems with a deep transverse arrest. I've alerted Theatre—I imagine you'll want to try a Keilland's rotation with surgical back-up if necessary, so we've got the crossmatching under way.'

'Thanks—OK, I'll be with you in a minute.'

'Jo?' Anne's voice was worried. 'Jo, are you OK?'

She tried to inject some normality into her voice. 'I'm fine. I'll see you soon.'

She disconnected and put the phone down, sliding off the edge of the bed and straightening her clothes. She dressed in silence, her fingers trembling, and when she was done she looked up to find him watching her, a strangely detached expression on his face.

'I have to go—problems. I. . .'

There didn't seem to be anything useful to say, so she turned on her heel and walked out and down the stairs, letting herself quietly out of the front door.

It took a moment before he realised she'd gone. Suddenly galvanised into action, he ran downstairs and flung open the front door, but her tail-lights were just disappearing out of sight. He sagged back against the doorframe, his body strangely weightless, and stared blankly at the dark road until his eyes ached.

He realised he was suffering from shock, and went into the kitchen and made a cup of strong coffee, drinking it quickly before it was really cool enough. The too-hot liquid cut through his inertia like nothing else had, and he felt the shock receding to expose the raw agony left in the wake of Jo's stark announcement.

A hysterectomy. Fate was so cruel, he thought, as the pain washed over him, and what a wicked twist she had devised this time. . .

Something about it puzzled him, though—not what Jo had said, but about her manner, as if she was concealing something from him. She had lied, he was sure of it—but what about?

Fear clutched at his heart like a cold hand. What if it hadn't been some abnormality, but cancer?

'No,' he ground out, 'not again! Dear God, not again, please!'

He slammed the coffee-cup down on the sink and ran upstairs, pulling on his sweater and shoes. He picked up his jacket on the way out, and then drove like a maniac all the way to the hospital, pulling up in the car park with a screech of brakes.

He didn't pause to lock the car, but ran to the staff entrance, only years of training slowing his footsteps to a rapid walk. His feet took him along endless corridors past countless beige doors to another beige door in a blank wall. Glancing at the sign above, he pushed it open.

There was no one at the desk, the bank of computers glowing silently in the quiet room.

Scanning the room quickly, he made his way through to the huge racks of patients' notes in the area behind. Without a hospital number it might take him some time to find them, but it shouldn't be impossible.

He found the Hs, and then the Hardings, and then, eventually, Joanna Louise of Two, the Row. That was it. It was a slim file, the information sparse and to the point in Owen's neat but spidery hand.

Hands shaking, Alex scanned the pages for any mention of carcinoma or other cancer that could steal her away from him.

There was none, and relief washed over him, gradually replaced by a cold horror as his eyes focused on the pages.

'Ectopic pregnancy of ten weeks' duration, situated in the left horn of a rudimentary bicornuate uterus—

extensive rupture—haemorrhage—circulatory collapse—unavoidable hysterectomy to arrest haemorrhage. Dear God. When?' He scanned the notes for a date, and froze. Early November, four years previously. Just over two months after their meeting.

He closed the file slowly and slid it back into the rack. His baby. He felt a well of sadness for the lost child that was never to be, and then that was replaced by anger, anger with himself because his carelessness had resulted in that conception, and because of his carelessness Jo had nearly died.

No wonder she didn't want to marry him!

'What on earth are you doing here? You can't come in here—please leave, immediately, or I'll have to call Security!'

Alex looked up, dazed, and saw a small, middle-aged woman marching towards him with an officious frown on her worried face. With a huge effort he shouldered himself away from the wall and twisted his mouth into what he hoped looked like a smile.

'I'm sorry—we haven't met. I'm Alexander Carter. I just wanted to check on some old notes. You weren't at the desk, but I didn't think you'd mind——'

'Mr Carter!' Suddenly relief broke out on the woman's face, and she relaxed visibly. 'I'm so sorry, I'm afraid I didn't recognise you. No, I don't really mind, but of course you shouldn't be in here either, to be perfectly honest. You doctors tend to leave the notes in a shocking muddle if we let you in—much easier all round if you ask us. Er—did you find what you wanted?'

'Yes, thank you,' he told her, trying not to think of

what he had found. 'I won't hold you up. Thanks for your help.'

He left her and made his way to the canteen, sitting in a corner and drinking cup after cup of coffee while he watched the steady trickle of night staff as they came and went.

Maybe Jo would come in—she hadn't had supper. Even if she didn't, it probably didn't matter if he sat here all night. He wouldn't sleep now anyway, between the coffee, her revelation and the contents of her notes.

But he would have to see her, as soon as possible. There was so much to say. An apology, first of all, and then to reassure her that he loved her anyway and wanted to marry her, regardless. After all, they could always adopt. She knew, of course, that he wanted children. God knew he'd told her enough times.

In growing horror, his mind ran back over the number of times he had teased her for her sentimental reaction to a birth, the times he'd told her she'd be a wonderful mother, the times she'd told him, in her way, that it wasn't to be. What was her favourite expression? 'I'm not that kind of woman.' He felt sick inside. What had he done to her?

He might have known there was more to it than she had said. She wasn't a career doctor—goodness knew he'd met enough of them, and she wasn't one nor ever could be, thank God. But having said that, she was always professional and coolheaded, never letting sentiment cloud her judgement. The only times he'd seen her even remotely upset were at deliveries—and Clare Barrington's ectopic.

He groaned. Of course! No wonder she'd been so quick off the mark—she'd been there before.

He closed his eyes. How could he even begin to make her understand that it was her he wanted, and not a mother for his nameless children? That although he wanted children in his life, it wasn't a prerequisite that they were his own flesh and blood?

An unexpected shaft of pain struck him with the realisation that he would never now hold his own child in his arms, but oddly his grief was that he couldn't give Jo what she so obviously wanted, and not for himself.

Straightening, he glanced at his watch. Ten-thirty. He wondered where she was. Theatre, perhaps? He had to see her, to find out if she was all right—though God knew if she would want to see *him*, after all the pain he'd unwittingly caused her.

With a ragged sigh, he unfolded his long legs and stood up slowly, leaving the litter of coffee-cups on the table behind him.

Jo stood in Theatre, her mind focused on finishing the suturing job in hand. The Keilland's rotation had failed, due to a pelvic anomaly that had somehow escaped detection. How, would have to be resolved later. For now it was sufficient that the baby was alive and well, the mother, although having had a section, would make a good recovery, and Jo's hands and mind were busy to the exclusion of thought.

As she tied the last suture and straightened her aching back, the thoughts came thudding back, hitting her like bullets.

Alex.

All she could see was the expression in his eyes,

those gentle, intelligent brown eyes washed with the pain of a disintegrating dream.

He wouldn't want her now, and, if he said he did, she would know he was lying. She'd seen it in his face, in the shock and hurt and disillusionment as he'd watched her dress.

She looked up, unsurprised to see him standing there just inside the door. Somehow she'd known he was there, had been there for some minutes, watching her quietly, his expression carefully blank.

She walked towards the door, reluctant to talk to him but unable to ignore his presence.

As she drew level with him his hand came out and rested lightly on her arm.

'Everything OK?' he asked gruffly.

'The op was fine,' she told him.

'That wasn't what I asked.'

She met his eyes then, and noticed the strain. There was a bitter twist to his mouth as he waited for her to answer.

She sighed and pulled off her gloves and mask, shaking her hair free of the cap.

'I'll be fine. How about you?'

He gave a derisive snort. 'Don't pretend to care, Jo,' he said roughly. 'We need to talk.'

'No, we don't,' she told him calmly. 'There's nothing more to say. Nothing's changed. I never did agree to marry you, so you don't need to find a reason to back out. Excuse me.'

She thrust the door open and pushed past him, leaving him standing there alone. She went into the showers and stood for endless minutes under the scalding water, hoping it would wash away the ache that had settled in her heart.

Secretly she had hoped he would say something—anything!—that would indicate that it didn't matter to him, but he hadn't. God knew what he wanted to say to her, but, seeing the bitterness in his eyes, she was quite sure she didn't want to hear it.

He was waiting, of course, apparently checking on the progress of the patient in Recovery but actually hanging about waiting for her with a determined set to his mouth that brooked no argument.

'Let's go to your office,' she said with a sigh.

They travelled down in the lift in silence, a gap between them a mile wide, and when he held the door of his office for her she went through it carefully, avoiding touching him.

'Sit down,' he said tersely, and she did, her feet aching after the long day, her body screaming its need for rest.

Alex paced to the window and stood there, staring out into the dark night. She could see his reflection in the window, and after a few seconds she realised he was watching her.

She looked away.

'You wanted to talk to me,' she said flatly.

'Yes.' He paused, and then his breath came out in a gust as he turned. 'I went to Medical Records and looked up your file.'

Her eyes flew up, her temper suddenly at flashpoint, and then she saw the look on his face and her anger drained away. 'I thought you would,' she sighed.

'I'm sorry. It was unforgivable, but I knew you were lying, and I had to know why. I thought perhaps you'd had cancer—I wondered if the reason you wouldn't marry me was because you knew you were dying. . .'

He turned back to the window, his shoulders rigid. 'Of course, I realise now why you won't marry me, and I won't press you. I can quite understand. It wouldn't be possible, would it, feeling like that?

'I just wanted the chance to apologise for what I did to you—if I had only thought to ask if you were on the Pill, it need never have happened. I just assumed—hell, you're a very sensual woman. It would have been a miracle if you weren't protected.'

'It wasn't your fault,' she said gently.

'Of course it was—I should have thought—I should have asked—damn it, Joanna, I should have taken precautions anyway!'

She laughed, a hollow, sad little sound in the quiet room. 'To protect yourself from me? I could have given you HIV, Alex. Did you think of that?'

'I didn't care. All I could think of was getting close to you, holding you in my arms and burying myself in you. I would have died content at that moment. I had no future that I cared to consider.'

She met the reflection of his eyes. 'And now?'

'None without you,' he said honestly. 'I love you, Jo. I know it isn't enough for you, but I can't give you the rest. Fate's taken that away from us, but if you could ever learn to forgive me for what I did to you——'

'You did nothing to me, Alex,' she interrupted, unable to let him continue and talk himself into a marriage he would hate. 'It takes two to tango—I could have said something to you, but I didn't.

Anyway, would it have done any good? Did you have anything with you?'

He shook his head. 'No. No, of course not. It was the last thing I expected to happen that night.'

'Likewise, but it did, and it was no more your fault than mine, and it certainly wasn't your fault that I had a congenital deformity of my uterus!'

He gave a short laugh. 'No, I can't claim any responsibility for that, but if I hadn't been so thoughtless—damn it, Jo, you nearly died because of me!'

'Yes, well, I didn't,' she said with a wry smile. 'That's one of the advantages of collapsing in a gynae theatre.'

He lowered himself into the chair opposite her and swivelled round, propping his feet against the wall and watching her in the window.

'Is that where you were?'

She nodded. 'I'd just finished closing for Owen. I felt sick, had a stabbing pain and passed out. When I woke up it was all over.'

'Have you seen your notes?' he asked.

'No.'

'You haemorrhaged.'

'I know.'

'Badly. If you'd been anywhere else, you probably wouldn't have made it.'

'But I wasn't, and I did, and it is not your fault,' she told him with studied emphasis.

'Nevertheless, it was partly my responsibility, and I can quite see why you hate me——'

Her head snapped up. 'I don't hate you, Alex,' she said softly.

'Then why the hell won't you marry me?'

'Oh, God, how dense are you?' she muttered, running her hands through her hair. 'I can't give you children, Alex. In time, you'll get over me and find someone else——'

'I'll never get over you, Jo. There'll never be another woman—not now.'

'That's ridiculous,' she argued. 'You've got over Cathy, haven't you? Or have you? Perhaps you're still in love with her, or maybe you never really loved her at all?'

'Cathy's dead,' he said harshly, 'and I did love her. I loved her wildly, passionately—but she's gone. I had no reason to believe that our marriage was going to be anything other than idyllic, but it wasn't to be. You can't guarantee anything in this life, Jo. What makes you think I'll find someone else and settle down and have my two point four kids without anything going wrong?'

'Well, the statistics must be on your side,' she reasoned.

He snorted. 'I'm glad something is,' he said bitterly. 'God knows fate isn't.' He sighed and dropped his feet to the floor, turning to face her. 'Look, Jo, I want children, I admit that, but they don't have to be mine. I've got nothing to prove by getting a woman pregnant—any fool can do that. Look at Damien and Karen, at their tender age! What does it prove? Nothing! There are plenty of children out there desperate for a loving home, and you'd be marvellous with them. I'm only more sorry than I can say that you'll never know the joy of bearing your own child, but from my point of view I have no urge to found a dynasty——'

'What about your dream?' she said quietly.

'What?'

'Your dream, Alex. A house full of children and grandchildren, growing old with your wife while the next generation ebb and flow around you. It means a lot to you. Please don't be noble. I won't marry you.'

'But I love you——'

'No, Alex. I'll make a deal. I'll have an affair with you—no strings, just a straightforward, adult relationship. Then you'll be free to go at any time.'

'No.'

'Why not?'

'Because it's not what I want. I'm holding out for marriage, Jo.'

'Then you'll hold out forever, because I won't marry you, Alex, not till hell freezes over. I know I can never be a part of your dream, but at least I can give you another chance at it.'

She stood up slowly and turned towards the door, but he was there before her, his face racked with anguish.

'For God's sake, Jo, don't do this to us!' he pleaded.

She forced herself to meet his eyes. 'Let me go, Alex,' she said quietly.

'No,' he murmured, 'not yet,' and he reached for her, his hands cupping her cheeks, his lips hard and demanding as he sought her response.

He nudged one leg between hers, and her traitorous body leant into him, her hands sliding round his waist to flatten against the solid column of his spine as the heat flowed from his lips and pooled low down in her body against the insistent pressure of his thigh.

She rubbed her breasts against the hard wall of his chest, and his hands left her face and drifted down to cup the aching fullness. A soft moan rose in her throat, and he squeezed gently and let her go.

She could hardly stand, her legs weak, her heart pounding like a steam-hammer, her breathing fast and tortured.

'Damn you,' she whispered, and, turning on her heel, she opened the door.

'If you change your mind, you know where to find me,' he told her.

She closed the door behind her and leant against the wall until her breathing steadied and the strength returned to her legs. Then she walked away, her only comfort the knowledge that he had been just as badly affected by the kiss.

It was cold comfort.

CHAPTER EIGHT

JO AVOIDED Alex whenever possible in the weeks that followed. As October faded into November and the leaves turned colour on the trees, she finished tidying up her garden and bought a book on cross-stitch, several pieces of cloth and a dozen skeins of thread in various shades.

About three weeks into November she finally settled down to tackle a sampler. It held her interest for about an hour before she was frustrated by her inability to concentrate.

The trouble was, of course, that, although she was avoiding him, Alex was doing nothing to avoid her, and she found herself in his company more times than coincidence would justify.

He was always politely friendly, always considerate as a boss, but he was always *there*, clogging up her life and messing around with her concentration.

She hurled the cross-stitch book across her little sitting-room and got up, frustration etched in every line of her body. And of course she was frustrated, desperately, and Alex went to great lengths to maintain that frustration at screaming pitch.

He never lost an opportunity to brush against her, and his eyes bathed her with that subtle mix of appreciation and humour that made her want to scream—or throw herself into his arms.

Which was, of course, precisely what he wanted.

Well, he isn't going to have it! she railed as she prowled round the house. Or me!

The phone rang, penetrating the fog of her ill temper. She considered ignoring it, but her conscience got the better of her and she picked it up.

It was Anne Gabriel, on call that night, to say that Sally Price, the widow with the cervical suture and the lousy obstetric history, had been admitted with contractions.

'I know you aren't on call, but I was sure you'd want to know,' Anne told her.

'Absolutely, Annie. Right, I'll come in. Start her on Salbutamol——'

'Alex has already done it—well, he was here. I could hardly tell him to shove off and let you deal with it, could I?'

Jo sighed. 'OK—well, look, I'll still come in and see her. I'll be with you in a minute.'

She found Anne on the ward with Sally Price, checking her contractions and monitoring the baby's heartbeat.

'Hello, Sally,' she said cheerfully, and perched on the edge of the bed. 'How you are doing?'

'Oh—hello, Dr Harding. I'm OK—well, I was, until this started up.'

Jo grinned. 'No problem—if we can keep you going a little longer, all well and good, but if not it really doesn't matter very much now. How many weeks are you?'

'Twenty-nine.'

She nodded. 'That's fine. We have much younger babies than that surviving these days. Techniques have improved enormously, and we have an excellent special care baby unit if you need it.'

Sally smiled half-heartedly. 'I can't believe I will,' she said, and her voice was heavy with despair.

'Rubbish,' Jo told her firmly, 'you'll both be fine. Now stop fretting, lie still and relax as much as possible, and we'll see if we can't settle all this down again.'

Jo and Anne walked together to the ward office while Anne filled Jo in on the treatment already prescribed.

'Alex has put her on Salbutamol, as you know, just to see if we can't get her to hang on, but I don't think he's really worried. He's arranged an ultrasound scan of the baby and the placental flow, and if all looks good I think he'll probably want to take the suture out and let nature take its course. He's started her on betamethasone to boost the baby's surfactant, to avoid the possibility of respiratory distress—hopefully it'll have time to work.'

Jo nodded, scanning the notes. 'What about special care? Have you alerted the paediatrician?'

'Yes, Maggie's on tonight,' Anne confirmed. 'She'll come down and look at the scan, and no doubt she'll get Peter Travers in if she's worried.'

Jo sighed and dropped into a chair. 'We'd better get him in for the delivery. We can't afford a mistake on this one, Annie—it's her last chance.'

Anne perched on the edge of the desk and looked at Jo worriedly. 'Talking of last chances,' she began tentatively, 'I know it's none of my business, but you and Alex——'

'You're right, Anne,' Jo said, her voice harsher than

she had intended. 'It is none of your business. Bleep me if you need me—I'll go and get some supper.' She stood abruptly and walked out, leaving Anne shaking her dark head in dismay.

Jo walked down the ward, hands stuffed into the pockets of her white coat, preoccupied with the problem of Sally Price and her baby. What if special care failed to save the baby? What if, after all the medical advances and technology were brought to bear, it still failed? Suddenly the odds seemed unbelievably long.

It was only when she bumped into Maggie Wells in the canteen and discussed it with her that she got the whole thing back into perspective.

'Come on, Jo!' she said with a grin. 'Twenty-nine weeks? Piece of cake, old thing, piece of cake. It'll be one and a half kilos, probably, or thereabouts—no problem. It's the very low birthweight babies—under a kilo—that we worry about these days. This'll be a breeze.'

After that she relaxed enough to eat her tortured salad and made her way back to the ward in a much more optimistic frame of mind.

Alex, of course, was there, but his presence was comforting, taking the pressure off her so that it was no longer her decision to remove the suture or not.

He was as perceptive as always, drawing her aside after a while to ask if she was all right.

She shrugged. 'Just worried about the baby.'

'Because it's her last chance? Don't worry, Jo, everything's looking good for her. I won't blow it.'

'May I stay?'

'Of course—do you want to take her over?'

'No, I——' She met his eyes, her own filled with

doubt. 'I'm not confident I'd make the right decision. What if I was wrong?'

He sighed. 'What if I'm wrong? We can only do our best. If we can stop her labour easily, we will. If not, I'd rather let her proceed if everything else looks good. She's in excellent health—a little depressed, but that's quite natural as she's been recently bereaved. Having the baby to care for will probably do her a power of good.'

He reached out and took her hand, giving it a reassuring squeeze. 'I'll carry on if you want, but I think she might well prefer you to conduct her labour.'

Jo swallowed and nodded. His touch was doing strange things to her, transmitting his confidence at the same time as it teased her senses. And that she could do without! She pulled her hand away.

'Fine. If it comes to that, I'd be happy to do it. Until then, I may as well go home if you're in the hospital anyway. It only takes me six minutes to get here.' And she could do with the breathing room.

As if he understood that, he smiled self-mockingly and waved her away.

'Go on,' he taunted gently. 'Run away if you must. I'll call you as soon as there's any change.'

She made her escape while the going was good.

The call came four hours later, as she was nodding off over a frightful old black and white film on the television.

'Jo? It's Alex.'

'How is she?'

'Her uterus won't settle, and her contractions are becoming more established. The scan showed the baby's a good size, and the placental flow is excellent, so we should have a healthy infant to deal with. I'm taking her up to Theatre now to remove the suture.'

Jo glanced at her watch. Nearly one o'clock. 'I'll join you,' she told him, putting the phone down as she grabbed her coat and shoved her feet into her shoes.

Within five minutes she was turning into the hospital car park, and two minutes later she was in Theatre where Alex, gowned and masked, had already begun to remove the suture. Jo stationed herself beside Sally and squeezed her hand.

'How are you doing, Mrs Price?' Alex asked at one point.

'OK—hurts a bit.'

'Sorry—I'm afraid it will, but it won't be long now.'

A moment later he withdrew the suture, a thick piece of silk cord, and Sally sighed with relief.

Immediately her cervix started to dilate.

'Well, that's certainly ripe,' he said, one eyebrow quirked above his mask. 'I don't think you'll be in labour very long. Right, let's get you back down to the delivery-room.'

He stripped off his gloves and pulled off the mask and hat, and Jo saw a wave of weariness cross his features in the unguarded moment before he glanced up and smiled at her.

'OK?' he asked.

'Yes—fine. Shall we go down?'

'Good idea.'

They went down in the theatre lift with Sally, and after that events progressed rapidly.

By two o'clock her cervix had dilated completely, and Jo gave her a pudendal block to numb the perineal area so they could give her an episiotomy and use forceps to cradle the baby's fragile head during delivery to guard against a skull fracture.

At two twenty-seven, only an hour after they had removed the suture, Sally gave birth to a tiny but perfect baby boy.

As he gave a weak but unmistakably angry little yell, Sally burst into tears and everyone else heaved a sigh of relief.

Peter Travers, the paediatrician, was there and examined the baby as he lay on Sally's tummy, his tiny legs hitched up and his skin bright pink with temper.

'Fabulous—no problem,' he told them all with a smile. 'He'll be in an incubator for a week or two, then a cot, and he should be home in a few weeks—eight at the most. Well done.'

'Can I stay with him?' Sally asked anxiously.

'Yes, of course. We'll move you to a side-ward up on the same floor as soon as you're finished here, and you can help look after him—in fact, we're relying on it. He'll need breast milk—one of the special care nurses will show you how to use Daisy——'

'Daisy?'

He laughed. 'The breast pump. Don't worry, it'll all be explained. I'll take the little lad up and get him settled, and we'll see you up there shortly. Does he have a name, by the way?'

Sally's eyes filled again. 'I thought—Anthony—after my husband.'

Peter squeezed her hand. 'Good name—I'm sure he'd be very proud of you both.'

Sally nodded dumbly, and watched anxiously as they wheeled her baby away in the incubator.

Jo cleared her throat. 'OK, Sally, let's get you finished up and you can go and join him.'

The suturing took some time, and when she was finished Jo straightened up and stretched her neck.

'All done,' she said brightly, and Sally was moved to a bed and wheeled up to the side-ward on Special Care where she would be in the care of a midwife.

Stripping off her gloves, Jo rolled her head on her neck and kneaded the muscles with her hand.

Alex moved up behind her, lifted her hand out of the way and laid his warm hand over the taut muscles of her neck.

'Ouch. Come along to the duty officer's room, and I'll sort that out.'

'But Anne Gabriel's there——'

'No, she isn't. I sent her home, knowing we'd be here. There didn't seem any point in three of us hanging around. Come on.'

She went, reluctantly, and lay face down on the bed, her head telling her was she being foolish and her heart telling her head to mind its own business.

Which reminded her, she'd snapped at Anne earlier for being concerned. She must remember to apologise when she next saw her, although, after twelve years of friendship, Annie would understand.

Alex sat down beside her, his weight dipping the bed, and grasped the muscles at each side of her neck in his large, firm hands.

Her jumper chafed her skin, and after a few moments he slid his hands under it and up her back to her shoulders again, his touch like fire on her bare skin.

'Alex, I——'

'Shh. Don't talk, just relax.'

She gave herself up to the hypnotic caress, and stopped fighting the sensation, letting the waves of relaxation wash over her as he rhythmically squeezed and stroked the muscles into submission.

'That's more like it,' he said much later, and slowly, reluctantly almost, drew his hands down her back and covered her again.

She rolled over and looked up at him. His eyes were hooded, the light behind him hiding his expression, but she thought he looked strangely sad.

'Thank you,' she murmured, and was instantly cross with herself because her voice was husky with emotion.

'My pleasure,' he replied, and his voice was equally husky.

He was going to kiss her, she knew it, and so she struggled to her feet, tugging down her skirt and rummaging under the bed with her toes for her shoes.

'Running away again, Jo?' he taunted softly.

'Alex, don't,' she begged. 'I'm tired, and I really don't feel up to an argument tonight.'

He sighed, ran his hands through his rumpled hair and stood up, flexing his shoulders.

'Are you going up to see Sally?'

'I thought I might.'

'I'll join you—if I may?' he asked with a sardonic twist to his lips.

'Of course you may,' she replied harshly. 'You don't need my permission to visit one of your patients!'

He laughed. 'Forgive me, I thought she was your patient.'

Jo smiled reluctantly. 'Come on, let's call a truce and

go and see her. Then I really must get home to bed.
I've got two lists tomorrow.'

'And I've got to drive to London for a conference.
Yuck.'

'Who's speaking?' she asked as they waited for the
lift.

'Me,' he said with evident disgust.

'Record it,' she said lightly, 'it would be fun to listen
to it—no doubt I'd find plenty to disagree with.'

He snorted. 'No doubt. You usually do.' The lift
arrived, and they travelled up in silence, both busy
with their thoughts.

Sally was settling well, her baby snug in his incubator, a seething mass of tubes and wires connected to a
battery of monitoring equipment. Jo and Alex wished
them both goodnight, and then went their separate
ways, Alex to the spartan comfort of the duty-room,
Jo home, however briefly, to her own bed, to be
taunted by the memory of his hands, warm and firm
and supple on her skin.

The next day she arrived early and popped up to
Special Care to see Sally and her baby. She was sitting
by the incubator, her hand through the port holding
the tiny fingers of her son while Maggie Wells checked
the monitors and adjusted the drip.

'Hello, ladies—how is he this morning?'

Maggie looked up and smiled. 'Hi, Jo. He's doing
really well. Proper little fighter. He'll be fine in no
time.'

'Any respiratory distress?'

'No, none. He's really in excellent shape at the
moment, and we're all watching him like hawks.'

Jo turned to Sally. 'How are you today? Very sore?'

She shook her head. 'Not too bad. To be honest, I haven't had time to think about it.'

Jo smiled. 'That's good, but don't forget to get enough rest. You mustn't overtire yourself this early on; you've got a long way to go before you can take him home and it's surprising how much it takes out of you sitting watching a baby for hour after hour.'

'I'll be careful,' Sally assured her.

'You do that,' Jo said with a smile, and left them. It was a relief to see Sally so much happier, as if the birth of her baby had given back her reason for living— which, of course, it had.

Just then Jo thought she could probably do with a reason for living—a reason other than the fact that she lived from hour to hour for a glimpse of Alex, or a chance encounter in the canteen, an unexpected meeting in the corridor——

'Hi.' His deep voice grated over her nerve endings, leaving them janglingly alert.

'Good morning.'

'How are the Price family?'

She forced a stiff smile. 'Mother and baby both doing well, as they say.'

'Good. Right, I'm off to London. Wish me luck!'

They were outside the ward kitchen, and, with a quick glance around, he propelled her through the doorway and kissed her until she was breathless.

Then with a cheerful wink he was gone, leaving her nerves at screaming pitch and her legs like jelly.

She poured herself a glass of water and drank it, then went round to see her list patients who were due to go to Theatre that morning.

The day passed in a blur. The morning list was straightforward obstetrics—two elective Caesarean sections and a cervical suture—but Alex's afternoon gynae list was trickier, two D and Cs, an ovarian cyst, a prolapse repair and a hysterectomy for a CA cervix that had migrated into the bladder wall and affected one of the lymph glands in the groin. Her prognosis was not good, and, although Jo did her best, she was unconvinced that it would be enough.

As she finished the suturing a nurse came into Theatre and told her she was needed as soon as possible on the obstetrics ward.

She nodded, finished off the last suture and handed over to Anne Gabriel, stripping off her gloves and gown on the way out and dumping them in the bin.

She was on the ward in two minutes, still in theatre greens, and found the sister.

'You've got a problem?' she said.

'Oh, yes, Jo—young drug addict in early labour. No clear idea of the date of her last period—thinks it might have been some time in March or April. Looking at her I'd say April, but she's so thin and jittery it's hard to tell. She's been mainlining heroin for a year, but that's the good news.'

Jo groaned. 'HIV positive?'

The sister nodded. 'So she says. We've taken some bloods, but we're treating her as positive until proved otherwise.'

'Yes, I think we have to. It's too risky to do anything else. What's her name?'

'Angie—Angie Lloyd. She's a bit on the wild side.'

Jo smiled wryly. 'Surprise, surprise! OK, let's take a look.'

Angie was in a little side-ward on her own, her thin, grubby face streaked with tears. Jo perched on the edge of the bed and smiled at her reassuringly.

'Hello, Angie. I'm Dr Harding, and I'm going to be looking after you while you have your baby. Now first of all we want to do a scan to see how big it is, because I gather you aren't all that sure about your dates. Is that right?'

Angie stared at Jo and swallowed convulsively. 'Can't you give me something? God, Doctor, I've got to have something. . .'

'We'll get you some methadone, or perhaps pethidine, once we've got the tests under way. Let's have a look at you first.' She turned to the midwife, who was hovering reluctantly in the background.

'Has anybody done a VE yet?'

The midwife shook her head.

'OK, Angie, I'd just like to see how your labour's progressing, so I'll need to have a feel inside to find out how your cervix is dilating. All right?'

Angie's only reply was to plead for more drugs. 'Can't I have something now? Please, I can't stand it.' She was restless and sweating, her eyes and nose were running constantly and she was yawning.

'When did you last have anything?' Jo asked her as she examined her swollen abdomen.

'Last night—about eleven o'clock. I scored off this guy I know—sometimes he'll give me a fix if I sleep with him. I hate him, but it's the only way. . .oh, please, help me!'

Jo sighed and pulled on her gloves. 'Let me see how far on you are. If you're nearly there, you can't have anything, but, if it's going to be some time, perhaps you could have a small shot. I'm thinking of the baby, Angie. It's very small to be born yet, and it's going to have enough problems without being born flat because of narcotics.'

She turned to the midwife. 'Sue, could you bring some Entonox, please?'

'What's that?' Angie asked, eyeing the cylinder suspiciously.

'Gas and air. It may help. Sue will show you how to work it.'

Moments later Angie was sucking gratefully at the mask, and Jo was examining her to establish the progress of her labour.

She stripped off the gloves and dropped them into a specially marked bin, then washed her hands again before drawing the midwife aside.

'Right, Sue, she's about four centimetres—we'll do the scan and see if we can establish the age of the baby, then we'll watch her and see how she gets on. If we give her pethidine and she then has a rapid labour, then the baby's got even more problems. I daren't risk it. Do you believe in God?'

Sue grinned. 'Why?'

'Just pray for a quick labour,' Jo said drily.

Three hours later, when there seemed to be little progress and Angie was all but climbing walls for a fix of something—anything!—to satisfy her craving, Alex wandered in.

'Hurray!' Jo muttered. 'Here come the cavalry. Come, I need to talk to you.'

'And hello to you too!' he said with a chuckle. 'Problems?'

She snorted, and rapidly filled him in with the details of Angie's labour and sketchy history.

'And that's it?'

She nodded. 'The medical social worker's been up and found out what she can, which isn't much, and all we dare do is hold her down on the bed and hope she gets on with it.'

Alex sighed heavily and ran his hand through his hair. 'And to think I really didn't want to go to that conference! Believe me, it was a piece of cake compared to reality!'

Jo smiled. 'How did it go? Did you cause a riot among the radicals?'

He grinned. 'No, actually. Rather the reverse. I'll tell you about it later.'

He went into the ward office, shrugged off his jacket and pulled on a white coat, and joined Jo at Angie's side.

The midwife reported a strengthening of the contractions, and, sure enough, Angie began to progress rapidly after that. She was finding it all rather hard to deal with and Sue had another delivery to attend, and so Jo sat with her and talked and rubbed her back with lavender oil and generally proffered comfort as the time passed.

She learned that Angie was a foster-child, having been abandoned by her mother at the age of four. Her foster parents had been many and various, the last and longest standing a vicar and his wife who had taken an erring child under their wing and shown her the light, from what Jo could gather. Apparently it had been a deeply unhappy experience, and Angie had left 'home'—such as it was—a year before, going to London to find her fortune.

She had found, instead, a world of drugs and child prostitutes, of hopelessness and disillusion. At last, driven by despair and the advancing months of her pregnancy, she had gone back to her foster parents, and they had thrown her out.

For the last three weeks she had slept rough, scrounging food and shelter when possible, selling herself when there was no alternative, to feed her addiction and raise much needed cash for food. When all else failed, she had rummaged through dustbins outside fast-food shops for the left-overs.

She was more alone than anyone Jo had ever met in her life, and she found her heart reaching out to the rejected child who had become such a tragic young woman.

Alex came and went, bringing Jo cups of tea and checking on Angie's progress, and when at nearly midnight she went into the second stage he was there at the birth of her baby, so that Jo, with Sue, was free to offer comfort and support.

Maggie Wells attended the delivery because of the likelihood of the baby having all manner of problems— respiratory distress, drug dependency problems, low birthweight, possible HIV-related symptoms. 'You name it,' Jo said to her, 'the baby could have it,' and so Maggie came down and checked the baby over when she was born.

She was small for her 'guesstimated' gestational age of thirty-four weeks, but consistent with the condition of the mother. Angie was allowed a few moments with her before she was removed to Special Care, and all

she could say was, 'She's so tiny—she's going to die—
what have I done to her?'

As soon as she was tidied up she was transferred to
the side-ward next to Sally Price, and lay shivering and
vomiting and craving until Alex prescribed some methadone. After that she was quiet for a while, but by the
following morning she was raving and nauseated, and
giving everybody a hard time.

Jo went up to see her and found her tearful and
distraught.

'What's up, Angie?' she asked sympathetically.

'I've failed her,' she sobbed. 'The only decent thing
I've done in my life, and I've cocked it up and failed
the poor little rat—I love her, Jo, but what kind of
mother will I be to her?'

'Oh, Angie,' Jo sighed, and, gathering her up, she
held her while she sobbed out all the anguish and
bitterness of a lifetime.

After that she slept a bit, and Jo popped up to see
how she was doing at lunchtime.

She was sitting by the cot, which was in an isolation
ward off the main unit, holding the baby's hand
through the porthole. The baby was very twitchy, the
slightest noise or movement making her jump and cry,
and she squirmed restlessly as they watched.

'What will happen to her when I die?' Angie asked
Jo matter-of-factly.

Jo took a deep breath. There was no point pretend-
ing that she wouldn't die, in view of her HIV and drug
dependence. When was a matter for the gods, but if—
Jo was sure that was already determined.

'I imagine she'd be adopted. There are lots of people
out there who can't have babies, you know. Many of

them would be not only able but also very willing to give her a loving home.'

'But she's going to get AIDS,' Angie said as if Jo had somehow missed the point.

'Maybe. There's actually only a twenty-five per cent chance that she'll end up HIV positive, and even if she does it could be years before she develops full-blown AIDS.'

'And people could still love her?'

'Oh, yes.' Jo's face softened as she looked at the baby. 'She's lovely, Angie. Anyone with a heart would love her.'

They fell silent for a while, and then Angie looked at her hands and said, 'Are you married, Jo?'

Jo sighed. 'No. No, I'm not, although there's someone who'd like to marry me.'

'So why don't you?' Angie asked, with her curiously direct gaze.

Jo looked away. 'Because it wouldn't work, Angie. You see, he wants children, and I can't have any.'

Angie's face creased in sympathy. 'Jo, that's so sad. Couldn't you adopt a baby?'

'Maybe, if we wanted to, but I think he wants his own kids.'

'And what about you? What if you'd already got married when you found out? Would you adopt?'

'Oh, yes,' Jo replied without hesitation. 'Like a shot. I love children.'

'Even Amy?'

'Is that her name?'

Angie nodded.

'Yes, even Amy—perhaps especially Amy, because her need would be so much greater. But for now, and for as long as we can make it happen, she's got you, love, and you need to get yourself back on track and learn how to take care of both of you, for her sake as much as yours.'

Her bleep went and, with a comforting squeeze to Angie's shoulder, she left her to return to the steady bustle of the ward below.

It was late again before she went off duty, and she couldn't believe it when the phone rang at six in the morning.

'Hello?' she mumbled sleepily.

'Jo? It's Alex. I'm sorry to wake you, but we've got a bit of a crisis at the hospital. Could you come down?'

'What, now?'

'I'm afraid so. It is important.'

'Mmm—OK,' she mumbled. 'What sort of a crisis?'

There was a short silence, and then Alex said, 'It's Angie—she's drowned herself in the fountain.'

CHAPTER NINE

BY THE time Jo arrived in Alex's office, the room was already full. There were two policemen, the hospital manager, Mrs Cripps the medical social worker, the porter who had found the body, and Alex.

He came straight to her as she entered the room, his hand gripping her elbow reassuringly as he greeted her.

She was outwardly calm, but trembling slightly, and she knew Alex could feel it as he quickly introduced her to those present.

All eyes swivelled to her, their curiosity evident as they inspected her like a bug under a microscope.

She was glad she had paused long enough to drag a comb through her wild hair and apply a streak of lipstick.

The police inspector, a man called Wiggins, looked at her steadily for a moment and then said, 'I'm glad you were able to join us, Dr Harding. You see, we've got a bit of a problem.'

'You're welcome,' Jo replied, 'although I don't see how I can help. I hardly knew her.'

'No, well, she wasn't the sort one would want to know, was she?'

Jo blinked. 'I didn't say that, Inspector,' she said firmly.

He held a tatty piece of paper out to her.

'I wonder if you could shed any light on this, Dr Harding?'

She took the paper and glanced at it, her puzzlement giving way to horror as she read and re-read the carefully penned note.

I'm sorry, I know it's the coward's way out, but I can't live with what I've done to Amy. Jo will love her—she said so. I want her to adopt Amy and take care of her as long as she's got—maybe it's not long anyway, but I can't. Tell her I loved her—that's why I called her Amy. I'm sorry. Angie.

Jo dropped the note and sank into a chair that someone thoughtfully shoved behind her legs.

'Does it mean anything to you, Dr Harding?' Wiggins asked.

'Yes—well, yes and no. I was talking to her yesterday—she was asking what would happen when she died. I don't know if you've been filled in with the details of her medical condition. . .?'

The man nodded. 'And you said you'd adopt her baby?' He sounded sceptical.

'Well—in a way. Not——'

'So you told her that if she died you'd look after her child?'

'No—no, not in so many words—I can't honestly remember my exact words, but I did say that Amy would be adopted, that plenty of people would be more than happy to take her on. She asked if I was married and I said no, and then——' Jo looked up and saw a bevy of interested spectators.

'Inspector, could I talk to you alone, please?'

'Of course. You won't mind if my colleague stays?'

Jo glanced at the WPC and shook her head. 'No, of

course not. It's just——' She waved her hand at the crowd, and they faded away.

Once they were alone, she explained the gist of her conversation with Angie, ending with the fact that she had told her she was unable to have children.

'And you never at any time had any idea that she might be about to commit suicide?'

'No—no, of course not, or I would have said something to Mr Carter and the social worker, and tried to talk her out of it!'

'Even though her death meant that you could have her child?'

Jo was appalled. 'Inspector, are you saying that I deliberately encouraged that tragic young woman to take her life so that I could have her baby?'

He returned her glare coldly. 'Dr Harding, forgive me, I have to examine all aspects of the case. If it seems to me that you have deliberately set her mind at rest with the express intention of enabling her to kill herself with a clean conscience, knowing that her child would be cared for, then I have a duty to investigate that possibility.'

'You're accusing me of—well, almost of murder! For God's sake, I'm a doctor!'

'You're also a woman who can't have children and is naturally bitter as a result. You aren't married, the adoption agencies wouldn't even consider you, you've chosen a very strange field for a childless woman—one might easily infer that you have an obsession with babies. I find the possibility of your involvement very credible, Dr Harding—in fact, you should be grateful that she died by drowning and not by a drug overdose which you could have administered or made available to her.'

'How dare you?' Jo was livid. 'I find your presumptions about my character totally offensive! You'll be searching my house next for evidence that I pushed her into the fountain!'

He sighed. 'Your house is currently being searched by a forensic team, as is your car. We haven't got anything yet on which to arrest you, but I must ask you not to leave the town for the next few days. By the way, where were you last night?'

Jo was stunned. 'At home.'

'Alone?'

'Yes, alone. I live alone.'

'Unfortunate. Is there anyone who could testify to your presence?'

She shook her head numbly. 'Only my neighbours, but they sleep at the back of the house and wouldn't hear my car anyway. There's quite a bit of traffic through the village, even at night. A car wouldn't be unusual.'

'I see. Do you have anything else to add?'

She shook her head again. 'No—no, nothing.'

The WPC read Jo's words back to her, asked if they were a true record of what she had said, and asked her to sign her statement.

'Thank you, Dr Harding,' Inspector Wiggins said coldly. 'We won't need to detain you any longer. If you think of anything else you want to tell us, ring the station, please, or come down.'

They left, and seconds later Alex slipped quietly through the door and crouched in front of her, holding her icy hands in his own.

'Jo?'

She stared at him with sightless eyes. 'That hateful man thinks I helped her kill herself—even murdered her! They've searched my house and my car, and I'm not allowed to leave the town—hell, Alex, what's going on?'

She buried her face in her hands and breathed in deeply. 'I've never heard anything so crazy. Why would I want to do a thing like that?'

'For Amy?'

Her head snapped up and she met his eyes, her own full of reproach. ' "*Et tu, Brute*?" They're implying I'm off my trolley because I can't have children—he said I'm a prime candidate for that kind of obsessive behaviour. He thought it was odd I'd chosen obstetrics, as if it underlined my obsession. He didn't realise I do it in spite of not being able to have babies of my own, not because of it——!'

'Shh. Don't pay any attention. I know damn well you didn't do any such thing, love. I've got something pretty unpleasant to tell you, as well. You're suspended from duty until the coroner has been informed and has made a decision regarding your implication in it.'

'Dear God!' she breathed, her face echoing her shock. 'That's ridiculous!'

'I know, but the hospital has to cover itself. Don't worry, I'm doing what I can to clear you.'

'Can I see Amy?'

He hesitated. 'There's no reason why not, but I wouldn't. Any interest you show in her will be piled up against you at the moment. She doesn't know who you are, so it won't hurt her not to see you, but it might do you a lot of harm.'

'I want to go home,' she said quietly, 'but the police have been crawling all over it and I don't think I can bear it.'

'Come and stay with me. I'll take you there now. Once the Press get hold of the story you'll be pestered to death anyway, so you can hide out until it all blows over——'

'Or they arrest me!'

'It won't come to that, don't worry. Come on, I'll take you home.'

He placed a protective arm around her shoulders and led her out of the building to the car park. Her car looked just the same as usual, but she knew it had been tampered with. For a start, it was unusually clean and tidy. Oh, well, she thought with a slight attempt at humour, there have to be some benefits. Perhaps they'd cleaned the house as well?

'I'll drive my car and follow you,' she told Alex, and tried not to think of uniformed police crawling over her possessions, inspecting them for evidence of her involvement in Angie's death.

She was glad when they arrived and Alex led her into the house. It was all but completed now, and he sat her down in the breakfast-room end of the kitchen and made her toast and tea and watched until she'd finished every morsel.

Then he took her up to the bedroom next to his, found her an oversize T-shirt and told her to go to bed and sleep.

He popped back at lunchtime briefly, and again, unexpectedly, at three.

'I thought you'd like to know,' he said gently, 'someone saw Angie walk into the fountain and lie

down. It was one of the geriatric patients on the ground
floor. She thought it was a dream, and she gets very
confused, but then rumour filtered through and what
she was able to tell the police fitted exactly with the
coroner's findings. It seems she drowned herself some
time between three and four this morning. A nurse
confirmed seeing the elderly woman standing at the
window staring out at about that time. She was there
for some minutes, apparently, and was very restless
after that. And Sally Price saw Angie leave the ward at
about three, but she didn't think anything of it. She
said she thought Angie was going for a wander—she
was very restless and twitchy.'

'So I'm in the clear.'

He nodded. 'It looks like that. You may find you
have to stay off duty for another day or so, but any
question of your involvement in her death seems much
less likely now. The rest depends, I would think, on
character references, and I can tell you the unit is in a
riot today following your suspension. You've got a very
loyal staff.'

Jo swallowed the unexpected lump in her throat.

'Thanks, Alex.'

He went back to the hospital, and that evening she
got up and went and sat with him in the sitting-room
she had designed. It was a curious way to escape—sort
of out of the frying-pan into the fire, she thought,
because, although she was free of outside pressure, the
internal pressure from her emotions was almost worse.

The phone rang several times. Maggie Wells rang to
give her a progress report on Amy.

'She's still very twitchy, but we're sedating her and
she's not too bad. Are you going to adopt her?'

'How can I?' Jo asked, although she had spent all day pondering on the possibility.

Anne Gabriel rang to offer her love and support, and Clare Barrington to say that if Jo required a character reference she would be more than happy to supply one.

Then the Press started, and in the end Alex rang the hospital, told them to bleep him if they needed him, and took the phone off the hook.

The following day the papers were full of it. Apparently her neighbours had been persecuted by the Press and had said that the whole story was silly; yes, she had been there all night and there was no way she would do anything awful like that. No, she wasn't obsessive about babies or in any way unbalanced. Yes, she had been a perfect, considerate neighbour. No, her morals were impeccable. She wasn't a thief or a liar or a moral degenerate. What did they think of her suitability as a parent? No comment. Did they know she couldn't have children? No comment.

The hospital issued a Press release for the evening papers saying that her part in the events had now been established and she was totally without any fault or responsibility for the unfortunate death of one of their patients. They were unable to comment on the post-mortem findings—that was up to the coroner. The baby in question was currently a ward of court and would remain so until further arrangements could be made for her.

The headlines, of course, were scandalous. Some filth had dredged up details of her medical history and published the distorted facts of her ectopic pregnancy—fortunately Alex's involvement was not known—while a local paper, under the guise of loyalty and support, had published an equally distorted article about the mental strain of childlessness, playing on the strange psychological effects that it could have.

Then they found out she was living with Alex.

The hospital closed ranks. Michael and Clare asked her if she wanted to go and hide out with them at the cottage.

Jo laughed. 'And give them that little tidbit? They'll conclude we've set up a *ménage à trois*! Thanks, but I don't think I'd better! Maybe I'll just go home.'

But Alex wouldn't allow it, saying if he had his way then everything the Press said about their relationship would be true, and he didn't give a damn.

Then the letters started to pour in, both to the hospital and to the Press, all in her defence. Many were from ex-patients who were unanimous in their praise of her professionalism and humanity.

One which the local paper published was from Polly Gregory, the GP's wife who had been the first patient to use the birthing-room under his care after Alex had joined the hospital.

She condemned the Press, both local and national, for their scurrilous muck-raking, and gave great emphasis to Jo's obvious mental stability and gentle humour.

Dr Harding is evidently a caring, intelligent woman whose contribution to childbirth in the area has been invaluable. It is also my opinion that she would be a caring, intelligent mother, and I sincerely hope that her adoption of the baby is both allowed and encouraged.

It reduced Jo to tears.

In the meantime, she was spending all her spare time in the sheltered and hallowed security of the special care baby unit, sitting beside Amy and caring for her whenever she was allowed.

Maggie Wells often paused to chat, and Jo felt truly welcomed in the unit. She knew they were concerned that she was getting too involved with Amy, but none of them had the heart to send her away.

One day she found a book of names, and mindful of Angie's puzzling comment, 'Tell her I loved her—that's why I called her Amy', she looked Amy up in the book.

'Oh, God,' she whispered softly, 'it means "beloved".'

Alex stood at the window in his office, staring blankly out over the woodland.

He had been talking to Mrs Cripps, the social worker, about the possibility of Jo adopting Amy. The difficulties, it seemed, were almost insurmountable. Not least of the things against her was her single status, although her profession would help as it was possible Amy would have ongoing medical problems if she was, indeed, HIV positive. That would not be established until she was about eighteen months because of the presence of her mother's antibodies in her bloodstream, but the possibility was there.

The letter from Angie effectively giving Jo guardianship of Amy was next to useless as it hadn't been witnessed, but there was no doubt it was Angie's writing and the wishes of the mother would hold some weight.

It seemed the main problem was her status, and that,

of course, was a drawback he could do something about. He would have to live with the knowledge that Jo had married him for Amy, but perhaps with time she could forgive him for the horror of her ectopic pregnancy and learn to love him. Certainly, he thought wryly, they would have no problems in bed. Whatever her personal feelings in the matter, Jo's body was on his side.

He made his way up to the special care baby unit and found Jo in her usual place, perched on a chair beside Amy, her head bowed forwards.

He walked silently towards her and peered over her shoulder at the book on her lap.

'"Amy, from the French *Aimée*, meaning beloved",' he read silently, and closed his eyes.

How well named she had been. Jo, for one, loved her dearly, fiercely protective of her and hovering anxiously during every medical procedure.

And Amy responded to her, quieter when she was there, more relaxed, although now after a week she was less twitchy than she had been.

Alex looked down at Jo's bent head, her hair falling softly round her face. He knew she was crying, her heart torn in two by the knowledge that she would almost inevitably lose Amy to some other, probably more suitable parents.

God knew if he could pull this off, but, if he could, he would. What was it Owen Davie had called Jo? The joker in the pack?

Alex's mouth tipped in a wry, humourless smile.

It was time to play the joker now. He only hoped he could come up trumps.

*   *   *

Jo slowly became aware of Alex's presence, and she lifted her tear-streaked face and smiled at him.

'Hi,' she said softly. 'I've just been reading this. . .' She passed him the book.

'I saw it. Are you OK?'

'I don't know, Alex. I keep thinking I'm going to lose her soon, that any day now she'll have a foster mother coming in here and getting to know her before she's discharged, and then she'll go to someone who doesn't know anything about her and can't possibly love her as I do. She's going to die, Alex, if she gets HIV, and no one will have loved her and made her happy in that time. It isn't fair—there are plenty of single parents who do a wonderful job. Why won't they give me a chance? Because they won't, will they? I was talking to Mrs Cripps about it.'

Alex pulled up a chair and sat close beside Jo, his hand finding hers and squeezing it gently.

'Maybe not as long as you're single, but you've got a lot going for you otherwise. My offer still stands, Jo. I'll willingly marry you and help you fight for Amy.'

She looked away, her mind reeling. If they were married, it would be different—Mrs Cripps had hinted as much. But it would be so unfair on him.

'Alex, I can't let you do that, it isn't fair——'

'Why? What half-brained reason are you going to dream up now? I need you, Jo, but I don't seem to be able to get that through to you. Well, Amy needs you, too. Perhaps you'll listen to her.'

He stood, laid his hand on her hair briefly and walked away.

Half an hour later Maggie Wells came in to check on

the baby and found Jo still sitting there, her face serious.

'Are you OK, lovey?' she asked, slipping into Alex's chair.

'He asked me to marry him again,' Jo replied automatically.

There was no need to explain who 'he' was.

'Well, I think you should—but then, I always did, long before Amy came on the scene. He loves you, Jo. I've been watching him while you've been up here sitting with Amy, and it's eating him alive.'

Jo looked at Maggie, whose lovely pansy-blue eyes were concerned, and tried to smile. 'Do you think so? I'm so afraid he'll feel trapped in a childless marriage and then leave me—Maggie, I'd die without him if we'd gone that far. What can I do?'

Maggie shrugged. 'Marry him. I'm sure you're wrong. And anyway, with Amy it wouldn't be a childless marriage.'

'But we might not get her. What then?'

'That's a risk you're going to have to take, if you want him. Do you?'

'Oh, yes, Maggie, of course I do. I love him.'

'Then marry him, and fight for Amy together.'

Jo sighed. 'You make it sound so simple.'

'And I think you're making it over-complicated. It's a tragedy you can't have your own children, granted, but there's nothing to stop you and the man you love having a rich and fulfilling life with or without children, and there are plenty of older children who are desperate for someone to love them—look at little Angie! If ever a girl needed a mother, she did.'

Jo nodded. 'You're right, I know that, but what if Alex is doing this for all the wrong reasons——?'

'Jo, he's big enough and ugly enough to know his own mind. He's not a fool. He loves you. I must go and check these babes. How's Amy?'

They had a brief chat about Amy's condition, and then, with a last admonition to follow her heart, Maggie breezed out and went into the main unit.

Amy was sleeping, so Jo went down to the ward office, shut the door and rang Mrs Cripps. Luckily she was still on duty, so Jo slipped downstairs to her office.

'I'm going to marry Alex Carter,' she announced.

Mrs Cripps tipped back her head, smiled at Jo and waved to the chair. 'Sit down, Jo. Let's talk it through. Why are you marrying him?'

'Because of Amy——'

'Just because of Amy?'

Jo sighed. 'No, not just because of Amy. I love him; I have done for years. We knew each other in London—only slightly, but I never really got over him. Meeting him again stirred up all the old feelings.'

'And how about Alex?'

'Oh, he loves me, I'm sure, but I'm worried he wants children.'

Mrs Cripps smiled. 'Not as much as he wants you, my dear. He's no fool, and he realises how much Amy means to you. If he's asked you to marry him, take my word for it, he knows what he's doing.'

Jo shifted in her chair, unwilling to ask the next question but knowing she must. 'How much difference do you think it would make to the adoption committee?'

'Oh, a world of difference! Obviously they still have

to vet you as parents, but, assuming you pass their tests and are approved as prospective parents, then bearing the mother's wishes in mind I see no reason why they shouldn't allow you to adopt Amy. However, you must remember that they have to do what's best for her. Your wishes and feelings come a poor second to Amy's best interests, Jo, and it's most irregular for them to allow this sort of thing. You must remember, there are probably two dozen sets of parents on their list at the moment, and probably between half and a quarter of them would take a child with HIV. You aren't the only ones who would give her a loving home, and you may not, in the long run, be the best. I hate to say this, but you'd better be prepared for a long fight and the possibility of failure.'

Jo stood up, her mind reeling. She had had no idea that adoption was so complex or so tightly controlled. After talking to Mrs Cripps, she could see her chances of succeeding without Alex were so remote as to be negligible. As for Alex—well, as Maggie said, he was big enough and ugly enough to know his own mind. Her thoughts were for Amy.

Thanking Mrs Cripps for her time, Jo left the office and made her way to the car park. Alex's car was gone—presumably he was at home.

She drove back, her heart in her mouth. How would he take her announcement? Would he be pleased? Overjoyed?

She felt like a young girl on her first date as she turned the key in the lock and went into the house.

Alex was in the kitchen, cooking. Taking a deep breath, she walked in and stood in the doorway, her arms folded almost defensively around her waist.

He was crouched down inspecting the contents of the fridge. When he saw her, he straightened up and turned towards her slowly, his eyes wary.

'Hi.'

'Did you mean it?' she said without preamble.

'That I want to marry you? Yes, I meant it.'

'Then I will.'

'For Amy?' He had turned away, and his face was hidden. She was sure, however, that there was no joy on it.

'Yes, for Amy,' she said quietly.

'Fine. I'll arrange it as quickly as possible. Where do you want to get married?'

'I don't know—the hospital chapel?'

'OK. We can have a small reception in the staff coffee lounge afterwards. Friday do?'

She nodded, and then realised he couldn't see her because he still had his back turned. 'Friday would be fine—I've got a list, though.'

'I'll do it in the morning. That'll give you time to tart yourself up. Red or white?'

'Red or white what?' she asked, her mind on the wedding.

'Wine—we're having lentil chilli for supper.'

So that was it.

'Red, please,' she said tonelessly, and walked away, her heart heavy. God help them both if the next forty years were destined to be as inspired.

CHAPTER TEN

THE next few days were a hectic rush. On Monday night, the night of her capitulation, Alex disappeared into the study and so she phoned Anne Gabriel and told her she was marrying him on Friday.

Anne, needless to say, was absolutely delighted and was singularly horrified at Jo's lack of enthusiasm.

'We'll go to Cambridge—do you suppose Alex could wangle to cover for us both tomorrow afternoon so we can go hunting for a dress?' she asked.

'A dress? What kind of a dress?' Jo said stupidly.

'A wedding dress!' Anne shrieked. 'Really, Jo, I've waited long enough to see you two tie the knot—if you imagine I'm going to stand back and watch you marry him in some drab tailored suit, you're quite mistaken! Failing Cambridge, we'll go into town and see what's available locally tomorrow at lunchtime. I gather there's a new wedding shop in the Arcade——'

'Anne, really, it isn't necessary,' Jo protested fruitlessly, but Anne wouldn't take no for an answer.

In the end Jo agreed reluctantly and went and tapped on the study door. Alex was sitting at his desk, a scatter of papers in front of him and a glass of wine cradled in his hand.

'Yes, Jo?' he said pleasantly enough, but his eyes were guarded.

'I—I wondered if you could cover for me tomorrow

some time so I could go shopping with Anne Gabriel. She says I need a wedding dress.'

'Of course,' he agreed. 'I've drafted an announcement for the local paper—would you run your eye over it and tell me what you think?'

'Is it necessary?' Jo asked, surprised.

'I think so—may as well scotch all the rumours and gossip going on, eh? Here. And what about guests? I haven't heard you mention parents.'

'No.' She lifted her eyes from the paper. 'That looks fine. No, I don't have any parents. My mother died two years ago, and I lost my father when I was twelve.'

Alex regarded her thoughtfully. 'Who will you ask to give you away?'

She blinked. There was so much to think about—and Alex seemed to be taking it very seriously. She supposed it was sensible to give it the appearance of a real wedding, but somehow her heart wasn't in it. If he had only shown any pleasure or happiness when she had given him her answer. . .

'Perhaps Owen Davie would come back—I'll ring him. As for the guests—anyone from the hospital whom you care to invite. I don't have any friends outside the hosital—my neighbours, I suppose. They were wonderful through all the fuss last week. No one else. Clare and Michael? Anne, Maggie—that's it.'

He nodded, and jotted down the names.

'Take tomorrow afternoon off, both of you. I'll cover.'

'Thanks.' She paused, but there didn't seem to be anything to say, and his head was bent over his desk again, so she went out, closed the door and went to bed.

The following afternoon she and Anne Gabriel went to town to the bridal shop. Jo started looking at the severe tailored suits, but Anne steered her away from them and over to the rack of voluminous, frothy confections.

'Don't be ridiculous!' Jo scoffed. 'I'll look like an enormous snowman in one of them!'

'If I might make a suggestion, madam,' the assistant put in, 'you do have a very beautiful figure, and I think we have just the dress for you. Not many people could wear it, but on you, I feel, it would be perfect—what size are you?'

'Fourteen—except for my waist, which is a twelve.'

'Here we are—and it would appear to be in your size. Perhaps you'd care to try it on?'

Jo eyed the magnificent cream silk gown suspiciously.

'Jo, it's fantastic. Come on,' Anne said, and dragged her into the fitting-room.

'Sometimes,' Jo told her, 'I regret ringing you to say that that job was up for grabs.' But she pulled off her jumper, slipped out of her skirt and allowed Anne to help her into the dress.

When the assistant had settled it down over her hips and fastened the myriad tiny buttons up the back, and produced a veil and combs to confine her wild hair, Jo had to admit that the dress was spectacular.

The bodice and skirt were strewn with tiny pearls, and the stiff puffed sleeves were set into a wide, scooped neckline that was almost but not quite off the shoulder.

'Sets off your clavicle a treat,' Anne joked, and Jo rolled her eyes. The assistant smiled.

'She's right, actually. You've got a lovely neck and shoulders, and you really do look exquisite in it. It would be a crying shame not to take it.'

'She'll take it,' Anne said firmly, and Jo surrendered. It didn't seem worth worrying about, and perhaps it would bring a glimmer of the old Alex back. . .

She didn't even flinch at the price, and agreed also to matching satin pumps, a veil and mother-of-pearl combs without a murmur.

Then the assistant asked, 'What about bridesmaids?'

'Oh—it wasn't going to be that sort of wedding, but—Annie, how about Beth?'

Anne bit her lip. 'She'd love it, Jo. She adores you, you know that. Nothing would make her happier.'

Jo didn't hesitate. 'What size is she?'

'Age seven, because she's quite tall, but she's only slight.'

The assistant rummaged among the smaller sizes and produced a beautiful dress in a warm peach that was lovely with the cream of Jo's dress and would be delightful with Beth's dark hair.

'If it's the wrong size, we've got the one above and below,' the assistant told her. 'And we can do alter-ations—when is the wedding?'

'Friday,' Jo said, writing out the cheque, and missed the woman's startled glance.

'Oh, well, if you rushed it back to us tonight, perhaps we could still—let's hope it isn't necessary. And I do wish you the very best.'

'Thank you,' Jo replied with a smile, and then left the shop, laden down with packages.

'I think,' Jo said to Anne, 'that she thought I had a baby on the way.'

'Well, let's hope you have,' Anne replied drily. 'Home?'

Jo gave a humourless laugh. 'I think so. Then I must pop in and see Amy, talking of babies.'

The next day the ward phone rang incessantly. Jo was in Theatre all morning, but the canteen was buzzing at lunchtime and she and Alex were greeted with a hail of good wishes when they went in together for lunch.

She noticed that his smile seemed a little forced on occasions, and wondered if hers was as transparently insincere. If only he really seemed to care. . .

Friday finally dawned, cold and rainy as befitted the first Friday in December.

While Alex did her theatre list, Jo washed her hair and bathed and shaved her legs and generally pampered herself, but with a conspicuous lack of enthusiasm.

It didn't matter, because there was no one there to notice until Anne arrived later with Beth, so she sat morosely on her bed in the guest room next to Alex's and smeared moisturiser into her legs and wondered half-heartedly if she should bother with nail varnish.

She decided she should and had just put it on when Anne arrived.

'There are some flowers in the porch—did you know?'

'No, I didn't. Hello, Beth. Are you looking forward to the wedding?'

Beth nodded enthusiastically, her eyes drawn like magnets to the dress hanging on the front of the wardrobe.

'Gosh, Auntie Jo! You're going to look so pretty!'

Jo smiled. 'So are you, poppet. Shall we get ready?'

Anne helped Beth into her dress and did her hair in a neat French plait while Jo blew on her nails.

'Have you packed yet?' Anne asked.

'Packed? What for?'

Anne rolled her eyes. 'Your honeymoon, dippy!'

'I'm not having one.'

'Yes, you are. Alex told me to make sure you packed something warm and casual—small country town, he said. I think he's bribed the other firm to cover the weekend—even I'm off!'

'God help us all—can Maggie come?'

'On the honeymoon?'

Jo chuckled. 'No, *dippy*, to the wedding.'

Anne snorted. 'Try and keep her away. She says Amy's looking better today, by the way. Oh, and Owen's arrived. I saw him in the coffee lounge. He'll meet us at the hospital.'

'It's a pity I couldn't get hold of Jake,' Jo said thoughtfully as she applied her make-up. 'It would have been just like old times at college to have him here too.'

Anne went still. 'Yes, it is a shame,' she said quietly. 'Never mind. Those days are over now. Time to move on.'

Jo shot her a glance. 'He always had a soft spot for you, you know.'

'Mmm. Come on, Beth, let's finish you off and you can watch television while I help Jo pack.'

In no time they were ready and on their way to the hospital in the taxi, together with the flowers that had been delivered earlier.

Jo supposed Alex must have ordered them. There

were soft peach and cream roses and freesias, and the scent was wonderful.

'It's beginning to feel like a real wedding,' Jo said to Anne, and her friend tutted.

'It *is* a real wedding,' she scolded.

'Yes, I suppose it is,' Jo said thoughtfully, and immediately felt an attack of butterflies.

There was a crowd to greet them at the chapel entrance, and Owen stepped forward and extended his arm gallantly. He was formally dressed in a dark suit and grey silk tie, and looked familiar and very dear. His wife was there, pressing a handkerchief to her eyes and doing all the right things, and Maggie Wells, dressed in a soft wool suit the colour of her eyes, kissed Jo's cheek and wished her luck.

'You look absolutely fantastic,' she told her. 'You'll knock him out of his socks.'

Jo laughed a little nervously.

'All ready?' Owen asked, and she nodded.

'Yes—yes, I think so.'

As they entered the chapel, the organist began Wagner's 'Bridal March' from *Lohengrin*, and Jo's eyes sought Alex. He was standing in front of the chancel, his straight back towards her, and there was a man beside him who Jo didn't recognise. Her eyes flicked over him briefly and returned to Alex.

He looked tall, distinguished and somehow remote, and then he turned, and, although his expression didn't change, some nameless emotion stirred deep in his eyes and his mouth tightened.

Dear God, Jo thought, perhaps I shouldn't have worn this dress—I probably remind him of Cathy!

Her feet faltered, and then he smiled, a gentle smile

full of encouragement, and she took a deep breath and found the courage to walk the last few steps to his side.

Owen handed her over with due solemnity, and she passed her bouquet back to a wide-eyed Beth with hands that barely trembled. The words of the ceremony flowed around her without meaning, and suddenly the chaplain was pronouncing them man and wife, and it was over, they were married, and it was too late for cold feet.

They were ushered into the vestry to sign the register, and then the organist struck up the triumphant notes of Mendelssohn's 'Wedding March' and she was floating down the aisle on Alex's arm, a fixed smile on her face and her heart beating nineteen to the dozen.

The reception was far busier than she had anticipated—indeed, the whole wedding was much more of a wedding than she had envisaged at the beginning of the week—and Owen made a hilariously funny speech about Jo that moved her almost to tears, and then proposed the toast to the health of the bride and groom. That's us, Jo thought stupidly, and shot a quick glance at Alex, but he seemed remote again. He stood up and thanked Owen, and then thanked everyone present for their wishes and the shower of gifts that had been lavished on them.

'I don't know if Jo is even aware, we've both been so busy this week, but my study at home is stacked almost to the ceiling with gifts, many from people I, certainly, hardly know. It just makes me realise how very lucky I am to have captured Jo, when I realise how much you all love her and how highly you all value her, both personally and professionally.

'Last week was hell—I never want to go through a

week like that again, and I'm sure I speak for Jo too—
but, once again, we were overwhelmed by the strength
of your support and solidarity. I can only thank you for
your endless small kindnesses that made it tolerable for
Jo. I'm sure most of you know that in due course we
hope to adopt Amy Lloyd—whether or not that will be
possible remains to be seen, but in the meantime our
thoughts and love are very much with her in Special
Care.'

He took a deep breath, produced a smile, and looked
down at Beth.

'Talking of beautiful little girls, I would like to say
how very splendidly Beth Gabriel performed her duties
this afternoon—wasn't she lovely?'

There was a murmur of approval, and Beth blushed
prettily and giggled.

Alex smiled, his first real smile that Jo had seen for
days, and then his brother made a speech on Beth's
behalf, told scandalous tales of Alex's youth and recommended that the adoption agency had better not get
wind of any of it or they would consider him wildly
unsuitable.

It broke the tension, and in the general relaxation
that followed Jo slipped away with Anne and Maggie
to change in the Ladies'.

'That was lovely—I do adore weddings,' Maggie said
dreamily.

Jo was still slightly numb. 'It was much grander than
I had anticipated,' she told them as they helped her out
of the dress.

'Nothing less than you deserved!' Anne said with a
grin. 'Didn't she look fantastic?'

'Utterly,' Maggie agreed, 'but doesn't she always?'

Jo blushed. 'Shut up, Maggie. It'll be your turn next.'

'Huh! Who to, pray? There isn't a decent man within a hundred miles that my grandmother hasn't introduced me to, and have you heard the latest? She wants me to go on a far-east cruise with her. Says she might need a little medical help—my grandmother! She hasn't had a day's illness in her life!'

Jo and Annie laughed.

'Perhaps you'll meet someone?' Anne suggested.

'Be nice,' she mused, 'but I doubt it, and, anyway, what good is that? It'll either be some bed-hopping Lothario or an ageing Romeo who wants one last flutter before he pops his clogs—no, thanks!'

Jo's eyes turned to Anne.

'How about you? Colin Bradley bit the dust months ago, and still there's no sign of a replacement. What about Jake? He's single again. Maybe he still has a soft spot for you.'

Anne turned away and busied herself folding up the wedding dress.

'I hardly think so, after all this time,' she said firmly. 'Anyway, Beth and I are quite happy as things are. If I feel she needs a father's influence, I'll borrow Alex. It'll be good practice for him. And talking of Alex, don't you think you ought to be going?'

Jo's heart crashed against her ribs. Her wedding night. She had no idea what to expect, no clear indication of what tonight would hold.

A few weeks ago she would have had not the slightest doubt of the outcome, but during the last fortnight, particularly, Alex had kept his distance, politely but firmly shutting Jo out.

Not that she had tried hard to get in. She had too many doubts and fears for that.

Forcing a brave smile, she looked at her friends.

'OK. How do I look?'

'Lovely—go on, anyone would think you had first-night nerves!' Maggie said with a smile.

'Don't be daft,' Anne told her, 'they've been living together for a week or more! No one's *that* slow on the uptake! Now go on!'

They left the hospital in a shower of confetti and good wishes, taking Alex's car back to the house to collect their things.

They had a short drive to the hotel in the nearby town where Alex had booked the honeymoon suite for the weekend, and there was a moment of tension as the bellboy delivered their suitcases to the room and then left them alone at last.

'Dinner's at seven,' Alex told her in a strained voice. 'I don't know if you want to have a drink, or get changed first and go for a short walk?'

'I wouldn't mind a cup of tea,' she told him, 'I've got rather a headache.'

'Me too. Do you want it in the room?'

They both glanced at the bed, then at each other.

'Maybe downstairs?' Jo suggested, a tremor in her voice.

'Of course,' Alex agreed, and politely ushered her out of the room and down the broad sweep of the staircase.

They drank their tea, then took a short walk in the floodlit garden. The morning's rain had died away, leaving everything damp and slightly misty.

Jo shivered, and Alex solicitously took her back inside.

By the time they had eaten, Jo was at screaming pitch. Alex was being so polite, so charming, and yet so—almost forced, in a way, as if he didn't want to be there.

They dallied in the bar over coffee until eleven, but by then the tension was so overwhelming that Jo was sure it must be visible. It wasn't a sexual tension, more a hideous uncertainty of what the future held for them both, and Jo sensed Alex's reluctance as clearly as she felt her own.

'Shall we make tracks?' he suggested finally, and she nodded, relieved almost that it was nearly over.

'Would you like to go first?' he asked, indicating the bathroom, but she shook her head.

'No, you carry on, I want to take off my make-up and hang up my clothes.'

He nodded and, taking his washbag and dressing-gown, he went into the bathroom and closed the door firmly.

Jo sagged against the dressing-table. What was the matter with her? At the very worst he would make love to her, and it wasn't as though it would be for the first time.

But it wasn't that, and she knew it.

No wonder brides cried on their wedding nights, Jo thought, and wondered how Amy was doing.

Alex emerged a short while later, his hair damp from the shower, his legs tantalisingly bare.

'It's all yours,' he said distantly.

'Thank you,' she replied, and almost screamed. They were being so damned *polite*!

She showered quickly, not wishing to drag things out any longer, and then with a quick spritz of body spray she dropped her nightdress over her head and went out into the bedroom.

Alex was in bed, propped up against the headboard, his arms folded across his bare chest, and Jo faltered at the look in his eyes.

'I hope you don't expect to get away with that,' he said huskily.

'With what?' she replied, her voice a mere breath of sound.

'That. . .' He waved his hand in the general direction of her nightdress.

She swallowed. 'Sorry—don't you approve? I didn't know what you would expect——'

Her voice cracked, and she turned away. When she opened her eyes, they met his in the mirror, and she was stunned by the raw animal desire that blazed in them.

'Come to bed,' he commanded gruffly.

She lifted the sheets on the empty half and slid in beside him, lying down and fixing her gaze on the ceiling.

'You look like a lamb to the slaughter,' he said, and his voice was rich with disgust.

'I'm sorry, it's ridiculous, but I feel so nervous——'

'Why?' He eased down beside her and his hand brushed her cheek. 'You know I'd never hurt you, Jo,' he murmured. 'I'm almost afraid to touch you I want you so badly. When I heard the "Bridal March" I nearly turned round, but I didn't dare. I was so afraid of what I'd see, but then when you drew level with me I couldn't believe how beautiful you looked.'

He closed his eyes and drew a deep, ragged breath. 'I'm sorry, this is going to be a disaster, but I—it's been such a long time, Jo—nearly four and a half years.'

'Four and a half—what? But that means. . .'

'That's right. There's been no one since you. You're a hard act to follow, Jo.' He gave a shaky sigh. 'I did try once, but it was a humiliating fiasco. She was lovely, but she wasn't you.'

'Oh, Alex,' she breathed, and her arms came up and circled his shoulders, pulling his down against her. To think she had doubted his love!

His lips found hers and the flames caught them and whirled them out of control in a wild sweep that left them aching with need.

'Now, please,' she begged, and, as he entered her, she thought her heart would burst with emotion.

'Alex, I love you,' she said tearfully, and he froze, his body motionless.

'Oh, dear God, Jo, you have no idea how I've longed to hear you say that!' he said raggedly, and then he was kissing her with all the love and tenderness of four frustrated years, and, as the passion built and exploded around them, they clung together and drifted gently back to earth in the sure knowledge of their love.

Later, curled together and content just to lie for a while, Alex touched her cheek with a finger.

'I've hardly ever seen you cry, and yet you've had so much to endure.'

'Not any more,' she told him confidently. 'I'm sorry I had any doubt about your love, but I was so worried you'd come to hate me because I couldn't give you children——'

He laughed. 'Don't be ridiculous. How could I hate you when you're my whole world?' He fell silent, his arms securely around her, and then he said softly, 'I'm sorry I can't promise you Amy, but if there's anything I can do, any action I can take, be sure I'll do it to get her for you if I possibly can.'

'I know.' She squeezed his arms. 'I love her, Alex, and I want her more than I can tell you, but she isn't why I married you. I want you to know that. I married you because I love you. Amy just gave me the excuse I needed to be brave enough to do it.'

She wriggled closer. 'I can't believe I was so nervous.'

He chuckled. 'I can—I was terrified.'

'You?' She squirmed round to face him. 'Why were you terrified?'

'I had such a wonderful memory of that night in your arms, but I was so afraid that it wasn't accurate, that tonight would turn out to be an anticlimax——'

Jo's throaty chuckle cut him off.

'Be serious, Mrs Carter!'

'No,' she told him. 'I've been serious for days. I want some fun.'

He quirked an eyebrow. 'Really?'

'Really.'

'What about your beauty sleep?'

'What about my beauty sleep?'

He regarded her thoughtfully. 'I quite agree. You simply don't need it. I can think of something much more beneficial. . .'

Look next month for Maggie's story in RAW DEAL, the second book in Caroline Anderson's trilogy.

Love is in the Air...

Mills & Boon have commissioned four of your favourite authors to write four tender romances.

Guaranteed love and excitement for St. Valentine's Day

A BRILLIANT DISGUISE	-	Rosalie Ash
FLOATING ON AIR	-	Angela Devine
THE PROPOSAL	-	Betty Neels
VIOLETS ARE BLUE	-	Jennifer Taylor

Available from January 1993   PRICE £3.99

_Available from Boots, Martins, John Menzies, W.H. Smith,
most supermarkets and other paperback stockists.
Also available from Mills & Boon Reader Service, PO Box 236,
Thornton Road, Croydon, Surrey CR9 3RU._

Mills & Boon

Discover the thrill of 4 Exciting Medical Romances – FREE

BOOKS FOR YOU

In the exciting world of modern medicine, the emotions of true love have an added drama. Now you can experience four of these unforgettable romantic tales of passion and heartbreak FREE – and look forward to a regular supply of Mills & Boon Medical Romances delivered direct to your door!

❧ ❧ ❧

Turn the page for details of 2 extra free gifts, and how to apply.

An Irresistible Offer from Mills & Boon

Here's an offer from Mills & Boon to become a regular reader of Medical Romances. To welcome you, we'd like you to have four books, a cuddly teddy and a special MYSTERY GIFT, all absolutely free and without obligation.

Then, every month you could look forward to receiving 4 more **brand new** Medical Romances for £1.60 each, delivered direct to your door, post and packing free. Plus our newsletter featuring author news, competitions, special offers, and lots more.

This invitation comes with no strings attached. You can cancel or suspend your subscription at any time, and still keep your free books and gifts.

Its so easy. Send no money now. Simply fill in the coupon below and post it at once to -

**Mills & Boon Reader Service, FREEPOST,
PO Box 236, Croydon, Surrey CR9 9EL**

NO STAMP REQUIRED